DEBAUCHERY AND THE EARL

Gentlemen of Pleasure, Book 4

Mary Lancaster

ARE YOU SIGNED UP FOR DRAGONBLADE'S BLOG?

You'll get the latest news and information on exclusive giveaways, exclusive excerpts, coming releases, sales, free books, cover reveals and more.

Check out our complete list of authors, too!

No spam, no junk. That's a promise!

Sign Up Here

www.dragonbladepublishing.com

Dearest Reader;

Thank you for your support of a small press. At Dragonblade Publishing, we strive to bring you the highest quality Historical Romance from some of the best authors in the business. Without your support, there is no 'us', so we sincerely hope you adore these stories and find some new favorite authors along the way.

Happy Reading!

CEO, Dragonblade Publishing

Additional Dragonblade books by Author Mary Lancaster

Gentlemen of Pleasure
The Devil and the Viscount (Book 1)
Temptation and the Artist (Book 2)
Sin and the Soldier (Book 3)
Debauchery and the Earl (Book 4)

Pleasure Garden Series
Unmasking the Hero (Book 1)
Unmasking Deception (Book 2)
Unmasking Sin (Book 3)
Unmasking the Duke (Book 4)
Unmasking the Thief (Book 5)

Crime & Passion Series
Mysterious Lover (Book 1)
Letters to a Lover (Book 2)
Dangerous Lover (Book 3)
Merry Lover (Novella)

The Husband Dilemma Series
How to Fool a Duke

Season of Scandal Series
Pursued by the Rake
Abandoned to the Prodigal
Married to the Rogue
Unmasked by her Lover
Her Star from the East (Novella)

Imperial Season Series
Vienna Waltz

CHAPTER ONE

L
ORD CALTON PROWLED the perimeter of the dance floor. This was no fashionable town hostess's elegant ballroom, but the shabby, somewhat vulgar splendor of the Maida Gardens pavilion, where a public masked ball was underway. And Calton, dangerously bored, was hunting for anyone or anything to relieve his ennui.

He was not even sure why he had come. It was certainly not in any great hope, more that he could not bear another vapid evening of Town entertainments. Nor his own company. And a surprising number of his friends, both the fastidious and the rakish, seemed to have found a way to happiness that began here.

Calton neither looked for nor expected happiness. All he sought was distraction, and as usual, he was disappointed. The orchestra—surprisingly good—played incessant waltzes. Males and females indulged in the usual mating rituals. Certainly, they were a little less refined here, with a good deal more shrieking and even blatant groping than in Mayfair ballrooms, but the basics appeared to be much the same.

Perhaps he should allow himself to be flattered by the come-hither glances and gestures of several females. But in truth, nothing and no one tempted him into even breaking his stride. He continued to look around him, mask twirling idly around his finger rather than concealing his face, and wished he had simply departed for the continent a few days earlier.

"Perhaps you would care to dance with me?"

Calton withdrew his gaze from the madly flirting couple on the edge of the dance floor to the speaker, who had apparently stepped from behind a pillar to accost him. Surprised at last, he paused. The unconventional—some would say shocking—invitation had been spoken in quiet, not unrefined tones, and the woman herself, though shrouded in a dark green domino and matching mask, looked neither gaudy nor plain. Her hood had fallen back to reveal her hair, a riot of barely tamed auburn curls caught up behind her head and allowed to fall to her nape, apart from one ringlet which tumbled over her left shoulder. Whether by accident or design, the effect was rather fetching.

A weak spark of interest sputtered to life.

Under his assessing gaze, her chin lifted. "Is the question difficult for you, my lord?"

"On the contrary, I am tongue-tied by a different question— why on earth would you want to dance with me?"

"Perhaps I find you handsome."

The words were bold, yet spoken, surely, with a trace of self-consciousness. Testing a barely formed theory, he stepped closer to her. Her breath caught, and her body twitched as though she would step back. She didn't, though, which began to intrigue him. She had rather beautiful, dark eyes, strangely brilliant now that he had moved and the light from the nearest wall sconce shone upon her.

"Perhaps you recognize me," he countered.

"Are you so famous?"

"No, but you *my lorded* me without a second thought."

"Flattery."

"Like the compliment of handsome?"

"I only said perhaps."

Calton's lips twitched. "A singular approach, but oddly irresistible. I can barely wait for the seduction part. By all means, let us dance."

THE EARL OF Calton's arm snaked around Josephine's waist and swept her onto the dance floor before she was ready. Every instinct shrieked to pull away from him, to run. She knew him to be a dangerous seducer—he had even used the word seduction in a conversation that had lasted only seconds! And yet this was what she had come for. She would ruin everything if she ran screaming from him now. If she could not relax her stiff body and plaster a smile on her face. She had found him, asked him to dance, and he had accepted, so everything was going to plan.

She tried to force the tension from her body, but it was not easy. He was overwhelmingly large and his arm at her waist was like steel. He swung her almost playfully around to face him, and she felt the shock of his hard body against her. She jerked back to a more decorous distance and to her relief, he allowed it, merely took her hand and began to dance.

He was a good dancer, graceful, light on his large feet, and easy to follow. Perhaps the dance would be easy to get through, after all, and then she could invite him into the gardens for a walk…

"So, what can I do for you, madam?" he asked, more amused curiosity than seduction in his voice.

"You are already dancing with me," she pointed out, "which is exactly what I asked of you."

His eyes were oddly entrancing, a deep, distinctive blue in the candlelight and very steady. What with those eyes and his shock of dark blond hair, carelessly long for fashion, his attraction was obvious. She could see how her sister had fallen so easily under his spell. Josephine, however, was made of sterner stuff. And was well-warned against him.

"I have been here in the pavilion almost half an hour," he reflected, "and I did not notice you popping out from pillars to invite other men to dance."

It had taken her twenty minutes after spotting him just to work up the courage. "I did not wish to dance with other men," she said with perfect honesty.

"I am in danger of being overwhelmed by such compliments," he remarked, sounding anything but. "And yet something tells me you don't even like me very much."

"How could I?" she retorted. "I don't know you."

"But you want to, having merely glimpsed me from behind your pillar?"

"Something like that."

"Where are your friends, little bird?" he asked softly.

"Perhaps I came alone. As you did."

"You should not, you know. Maida Gardens is not safe for young ladies like you."

"Because of gentlemen like you?" she challenged.

A sudden smile blazed in his eyes and curved his lips, then vanished before she could even blink in its glory. "Partly. Though there are also the thieves and pickpockets and men even less scrupulous than I."

"Surely not," she marveled and won another of those flashing smiles, though this time only in his eyes.

"I am not a pigeon for plucking, you know." He spoke casually, but she heard the warning, nonetheless.

"You are timid?" she asked provokingly.

"Terribly."

"Then I wonder at your dancing with a strange woman who has the temerity to ask you."

"Curiosity was ever my besetting sin, and besides, if you saw her through my eyes, you would not wonder at all."

"Ah. Reciprocated flattery."

"Have we met before, madam?"

"Why should you imagine such an unlikely premise?"

"Because you keep avoiding the question," he said wryly. His hand crept up her back from her waist, making her shiver with a sudden surge of increased awareness.

I am not in his power, she told herself for the second time since accosting him. *He is in mine.* It did not feel like that as his fingers moved in her hair. Suddenly realizing he was untying her mask, she whisked her own hand up to his and caught it.

"What is the matter, sir?" she managed, coolly, and just a little huskily. "Don't you like a mystery?"

A subtle darkening of his eyes told her he was not immune either to her new tone or her words. His sensual lips curved. His hand, when she released it, slipped caressingly back down over nape and back, but at least left her mask in place.

His voice caressed, too. "Some mysteries—or their solutions—I find most…satisfying."

Suspecting there was rather more to his words than she understood, she eyed him with a mixture of doubt and hauteur that brought back the quick, dazzling smile that caught at the breath of the unwary.

"That look, however," he said softly, "I find most intriguing of all. Did you really come here alone?"

"I did."

"Why?"

He almost sounded concerned, which she did not believe for a moment. So, she smiled. "To dance with you, of course."

"Then we do know each other?"

She considered. "It would be more accurate to say I know *of* you. I have no idea what if anything you know of me."

"Then where have we met?"

"Why does it matter? Do people not come here to forget their everyday lives and be someone else for a night?"

That seemed to be a lucky hit. Certainly, she had the feeling he accepted it, for he said no more on the subject, but waltzed in silence for a little. On the other hand, without his arm seeming to tighten, she found herself held closer to him, the heat of his body radiating into hers in a way that was oddly exciting. She even felt the shocking brush of his hip as they turned, and knew with sudden, blinding clarity that she was out of her depth.

I am not in his power. He is in mine....
What imbecile would believe that?
I do and it's true. It will *be true.*

"I think that one-second pause in the music was the break between dances," he murmured. "May I have the pleasure of another? Or have you had enough of my noble and *perhaps* handsome company?"

She licked her suddenly dry lips. "It is so very warm in here. Perhaps you would be good enough to escort me into the fresh air?"

His face was unreadable, but he did not appear to dislike the idea. He merely offered his arm as though he were indeed the perfect gentleman he was supposed to be. He guided her through the milling throngs on the dance floor and the boisterous group of people lining the way to the nearest door. Her heart beat so loudly, she thought he must hear it.

Although he did not appear to be nervous, he was watchful as they walked into the cool, fresh, autumn evening. Unfortunately, since the weather was so mild, there were too many other people around the gardens, dancing, laughing, flirting, and playing questionable hiding games. She had imagined it would be easy to be alone with him here, and it clearly was not. Nor could she do what she had to with an audience.

She stole a glance at him as they strolled along the path, and her stomach gave a funny little dive. Nerves, no doubt. Curiously, the sensation was not unpleasant. Nor was he remotely unpleasant to look at. In fact, she understood exactly why Helena had fallen for him.

He was undeniably handsome, and there was a wicked mischief in his smile, an intriguing contrast to the knowing, jaded weariness behind his eyes. The latter should not have been remotely attractive, and yet it was. Perhaps it inspired impossible hope in gullible females that *she* would be the one, the lasting happiness of his life to banish all others. Even though it was clear to the meanest intelligence that the only happiness he sought was very, very temporary.

The throngs began to thin as they walked farther away from the pavilion. His arm moved and slipped around her waist, and she allowed it because it gave her the excuse to be alone with him.

"Look at me," he murmured, his fingers beginning to caress her waist.

Unwarily, she cast him another upward glance, and his lips swooped down, planting a quick kiss on hers. Immediately, all words, all plans flew out of her mind. She could only stare up at him dumbly.

He came to a halt, turning her to face him. "Is this what you want? To be alone with me?"

"Yes," she managed, since that at least was honest. But his arm brought her to rest against his body, all hardness and muscle, and heat surged through her veins. *Now. Do it now!*

She glanced up and down the path. A couple walked ahead of them. Two more laughed and chattered behind them.

"It doesn't matter," he said, low. "You are masked, and no one knows you." His lips smiled as they drew nearer to hers again. "Not even I."

In panic, she dodged backward, whisking herself out of his arms with what she hoped was a coquette's laughter. "You are forward, sir." She hurried on up the path, where no one was now visible ahead, and with trembling fingers, began to open her reticule.

"I can be," he allowed, falling into step beside her and matching his step to hers. "So can you, between bouts of missishness. But something tells me you are not yet ready to play the game."

"Game?" she repeated. God knew this was no game to her.

"If you wish to speak to me on some matter I am too stupid to comprehend, we are private enough here. But on the whole, I believe I should return you to the ballroom or take you to the hackney stand."

Dear God, did he expect her to believe in his chivalry? Why

would he even try? Except as another means to get around her.

"No," she said firmly, her fingers scrabbling desperately inside her reticule. How could something so large be so wretchedly elusive? "Perhaps there is—" She broke off, her fingers closing at last around the article she sought. But a furtive glance ahead showed her no privacy any longer, but a large building with a liveried doorman outside it and several coachmen or grooms approaching them.

She let the reticule fall and dangle from her wrist, the strings closing it for her. "What place is that?"

The servants passed them with a quick, respectful tug of the forelock, which Calton acknowledged with a nod.

"Renwick's Hotel. I wondered if that was where you were taking me. You are not staying there?"

Hotel… Were there not more possibilities here? On the other hand, if she were seen going inside with him….

I am masked. I am safe. And I am not in his power…

"I am not staying there."

"I am," he said.

He would have private rooms of his own. It could be perfect.

"Shall we go in?" he asked. "Or would you rather go back to the ball?"

For some reason, it bothered her that he was still giving her that choice. But then, women came easily to him. There were plenty more at the ball. Why should he exert himself over one, if there were several just waiting to fall into his lap? Outrage surged once more.

"Let us go in."

He inclined his head, and raised his hand, drawing the hood of her domino up over her hair like a cowl. His lips twitched, as though they were sharing a joke, and her stomach performed its strange dive once again. The man, she thought grimly, was damnably attractive.

She took his proffered arm once more, and they walked along the front terrace to the doorman, who obligingly ushered them inside. She was almost relieved to see a large, tastefully decorated hall, well-lit and empty, save for a few men wrestling trunks toward a back staircase.

"My lord," said someone they passed. She was afraid to look and kept her gaze straight ahead. Calton gave an amiable nod without stopping, and then they were ascending the sweeping staircase lit from wall sconces, and she had the feeling she was falling deeper and deeper into a situation over which she had no control.

I do. He is in my power. He just does not know it yet...

He swept her along a hallway, also comfortingly well-lit, and kept going. She had to force herself to concentrate, so that when they left again, she would be sure of the way and not be tricked.

He halted and she released his arm to let him take a key from his pocket and open the door. Her already hammering heart gave an extra lunge as she stepped over the threshold and stopped in darkness. She felt him moving beside her and then the glow of a lamp showed her a large, canopied bed directly in front of her.

Her eyes slid away. While he moved around the room, lighting more candles until the room was, if not bright, then at least cozy. Cozy was not something she should even think about in his bedchamber. Pulling herself together, she walked further into the room and opened her reticule once more.

A hand closed over it, plucking it from her hold. She gasped in horror, though he only cast it onto the nearest chair without looking. His attention was all on her.

"And now, finally, we are entirely alone," he said.

"Your valet?" she asked nervously.

"I left him in Town when I escaped."

"Escaped?" she repeated.

"Figuratively speaking. I have not escaped prison, bandits, or foreign soldiers."

Gazing down at her, he raised his hands and pushed back her hood. Since he had separated her from her reticule, she allowed him to unfasten her domino cloak, although it felt very strange to have his fingers brushing against the naked skin of her throat. He had long, rather elegant hands, although his fingers felt slightly roughened, probably by riding or boxing or other manly sports.

Her cloak parted, but his fingers lingered. One brushed lightly over the rapidly beating pulse at the base of her neck. Her breath seemed to vanish.

"I would like to think my nearness moves you to desire," he said softly, "and yet... I cannot rid myself of the notion this betokens some less pleasurable emotion. Are you afraid of me, Madam Mystery?"

"Should I be?" It came out more as a croak than the careless rejoinder she had intended.

"No," he said at once. "I have already offered to take you back. I can still find a hotel servant to escort you, if you would rather, or to find you a room of your own here."

"Is this *kindness*?" she blurted.

His lips twitched. "Utterly self-sacrificing generosity," he assured her. "You intrigue me, Little Mystery, but you had best tell me what it is you really want. Before I begin to persuade you otherwise."

His lips fascinated her, more even than the heat that seemed to flow from his words. She could not understand how the movement of his mouth could express such self-deprecating humor along with such desire and something perilously close to the kindness she had accused him of. Besides which, the shape was pleasingly sinful, and the texture... He had brushed those lips against hers, so briefly she had had little chance to taste. She wondered how they would feel pressed to hers with more purpose, with the desire and persuasion he had been talking about.

She swallowed, forcing her gaze up to his. That was no help, for his eyes were drowning her in more knowing heat. In desperation, she darted a glance beyond him and saw a bottle and glasses on the dressing table.

"Perhaps a glass of wine," she said, hoping it didn't sound like a plea. "And I shall tell you all."

His lips quirked, but after an instant, he did move away toward the decanter. She had no time to analyze the bizarre disappointment that came with the flood of relief. She moved on trembling legs to the chair where her abandoned reticule lay and took from it, at last, the small, gold-mounted pistol.

"So," he said, his voice behind her and coming nearer. "What is it I might do for you?"

With a deep breath, she turned and aimed the pistol somewhat shakily at his heart. He paused, a glass in either hand.

She said firmly, "You will come with me and marry my sister."

CHAPTER TWO

GRATIFYINGLY, HIS GAZE fixed on the pistol.

"I will?" Damn him, he still sounded amused. "It seems a rather bizarre proposal. Don't you think she should have come instead? I have to tell you both I am not looking for marriage at this point, but I always listen to reasonable offers."

"*Reasonable*—" She glared at him. "You are rude!"

"I? My dear lady, *you* are standing in my bedchamber pointing a gun at me. At the very least, it is surely a breach of manners."

He started walking toward her again.

"What are you doing?" she demanded. "Stop!"

"Doing? I'm giving you the wine you requested." He was, too, holding one glass out toward her free hand. Even more bizarrely, she took it from him as though in a trance. "*Salut,*" he said amiably, raising his glass, and sauntered away to the bed. He must have been unbuttoning his coat as he went, for he shrugged it off and tossed it carelessly across the footboard, before climbing the step and lounging back against the pillows.

In panic, she followed part of the way, afraid of him getting away from her precarious aim.

He gestured politely toward the rest of the huge bed. "Please, make yourself comfortable, and tell me why you need a pistol to find your sister a bridegroom. I cannot imagine she is so very ugly, but perhaps she is a lackwit? Or merely a shrew?"

"My sister is neither," she retorted. "She is with child."

She had the satisfaction of seeing him pause once more, the glass almost touching his lips, just as though there were no pistol pointing at his heart. He lowered the glass again, his eyes slightly more wary.

"Is she, by God? And you think I am the father?"

"I know you are."

"How?"

"Because my sister told me," she said between her teeth.

"Then you had better tell me who *she* is."

She stared at him. "Are there so many possibilities?"

"In the half-year or so that we may be talking about, there are *some* possibilities, though no likelihoods."

"Are you adding insult to injury by calling my sister a liar?"

"My dear, until I know who the devil she is, I cannot call her anything at all. But do let us be done with the pistol. For one thing, I know you won't fire it."

"Will I not?" she said dangerously, taking a step nearer.

"I don't believe you are foolish enough, since it would bring the hotel staff crashing in upon us at the double, along with most of the guests. Closely followed by the Watch, no doubt Bow Street Runners, newspaper reporters, and a scandal delicious enough to keep the *ton* in gossip well beyond next spring."

He was right, of course. Firing would be the last resort only, but she had no intention of allowing him the point. *"My dear,"* she said in mocking imitation of his earlier words, "you have no idea how foolish I can be. But, of course, I am open to reasonable offers. For example, if you pick up your coat and give me your word that you will come with me to my father, then I might be persuaded. If you don't, who knows?"

His eyes gleamed with what seemed to be appreciation rather than chagrin.

"Hmm. Sadly, I do not respond well to threats. And you should know, to begin with, that I am not in the habit of ignoring my responsibilities. If your sister believes I am the father of her child, let her come to me, and I will do all I can for her. And finally, since you bring up the subject of lies, I am an earl and known to be a wealthy man. More than one woman has tried such false tricks on me in the past, although not since I was a stripling and expected to be easy pickings."

"I am not in the habit of ignoring my responsibilities." For the first time, doubt penetrated Josephine's outrage. Not that she imagined her sister wished to extort money from an earl—that truly was ridiculous. But that her sister may have given her the wrong name merely to throw her off the scent. That was *not* beyond Helena, especially when she would never expect her little sister to *do* anything about it.

So now, Josephine was in a quandary. If she revealed Helena's name, then if Calton were not the father, after all, he could ruin both of them easily. If she did not reveal it, then neither of them would be sure if he was the father of Helena's misfortunes.

Without meaning to, she found herself sitting down on the edge of the bed, though she hastily steadied the pistol again.

Lord Calton's gaze shifted from the pistol back to her face. "We are in a bit of a dilemma. Perhaps we need a less direct means of questioning. Did this—er…encounter of your sister's occur during the spring Season?"

"I am not sure," she said warily. "A little after, I think."

"And by your speech, you and your sister are both gently born."

She glared at him by way of an answer.

"Of course you are," he murmured. "And since she wishes to marry me—or you wish her to marry me—she cannot be married already. Unless… Is she a widow?"

"No."

"Then the child is not mine."

The ease, the relief with which he could simply cast off the issue that would ruin Helena's life and their father's, to say nothing of Josephine's own, and stigmatize an innocent child, infuriated her. The sheer injustice of men's lies and temporary pleasures outraged her all over again. Needing to throw something, she felt the object still held in her left hand and raised it to hurl at Lord Calton. She only remembered what it was she held when wine slopped out of the glass over her fingers, distracting her.

And suddenly something heavy landed on her, pushing her onto her back. The glass fell, and the pistol was wrenched from her hand.

Panting and dazed by the speed of events, she stared up into the face almost touching hers. Both his arms stretched up beyond her shoulders, and although he did not break his gaze, she heard the click and clatter of the bullet being emptied from the pistol.

She was pinned to the mattress by the weight of his body.

"Get off me," she said between her teeth when what she wanted was to smack him, hard.

"Where's the rush?" he drawled, easing up on his elbows in order to inspect her pistol. "Aren't you comfortable?"

She didn't trouble to answer that, and he did not seem to expect her to, for he tossed the empty pistol onto the bed beside her head. "Pretty little thing. Do you even know how to shoot it?"

"Of course," she said coldly.

"What a dangerous little creature you are to be out alone, offering intimacies to strange men."

She flushed, which had an odd effect on her body when he all but lay on her. "I offered to shoot you, not...to be intimate with you."

"Oh, I think you offered both, though I doubt you meant either. Which is a risky game."

Something seemed to be growing between them, in the region of her abdomen, something ridge-like and... *Oh, God, is that...?*

"And perhaps it is my turn to play persuasion." His voice had deepened, his eyes darkened, as they had in the pavilion earlier only more so.

"What do you mean?" she asked shakily.

He smiled with curious deliberation, and yet the effect was dazzling. In fresh panic, she seized his shoulders, but his head lowered inexorably until his mouth covered hers.

She had prepared for assault and was ready to fight like ten devils. But this was not remotely barbaric. This was slow and gentle and bewildering.

"What are you…?" she began against his lips, only to have them seal over hers in a more intimate yet still gentle manner. The inexplicable heat in her body, spreading outward from his obvious arousal, seemed to absorb the sensations of his kiss. Or perhaps it was the other way around. Either way, her mouth opened to the urging of his, and she had the insane urge to kiss him back, although she was not quite sure how to go about it, even if she wanted to.

She tried to speak again, but her words got lost in the silken warmth of his caressing mouth. His fingers sank into her hair and played across her face. He moved on her, stroking her with his whole body. And dear God, she loved it. When his mouth sank deeper against hers, her lips clung to his and her body arched up in confused wonder.

Something slipped against her face and vanished. His mouth loosened slowly, as deliberately as the kiss had begun.

"Now I could take you," he said huskily. "Show you the pleasure and intimacy I never knew with your sister. And you would let me. You would cling and cry out your joy in my arms. There are more weapons in the world than pistols, and you are not qualified to fight them. Come, it's time I took you home."

He eased off her and off the bed, casually picking up his coat and her pistol as he went.

Josephine, still dazed and stunned, took a moment to understand him. Humiliatingly, he was right, and that was from her original position of mistrust and even hatred. Her body had betrayed her, as perhaps Helena's had betrayed *her*. The sheer unkindness of his little lesson took her breath away all over again, as did the knowledge of her narrow escape.

She sat up in a rush and saw her mask on the bed beside her. Fresh humiliation washed through her, especially, when he sat down beside her and put the mask back on for her. His fingers touched her face, whispered amongst her hair. She sprang up before he did, her only aim to get out of there and away from him.

She snatched up her domino cloak from the chair, fastened it without looking at him, and turned to find him holding out her reticule.

"The pistol is inside. I believe I shall keep the bullet for now."

"Very wise," she uttered, grabbing the reticule from him and stalking toward the door.

His hand reached the key before hers did, but only to turn it anti-clockwise and open the door. She marched past him, and he said nothing, not even goodnight, though she soon discovered why. He was walking two or three paces behind her.

Since the passage was empty, she hissed, "I do not need your escort."

"Yes, you do."

She marched out of the hotel, more furious now than ashamed. Only when she approached the hackney stand between the entrance to the hotel drive and that of gates to the pleasure garden, did he walk beside her.

"You will not come in the carriage with me," she said low.

"I will."

"If you try to, I shall scream. Be aware, I have tricks which you are not qualified to fight."

A boy ran up to open the door and lower the steps for her. She sailed into the cab and closed the door herself. Through the window by the lantern lights of the waiting hackneys, she could see Lord Calton's smile, a little sardonic but also admiring. And then the carriage left him behind.

CALTON DID ADMIRE her. He also feared for her, going after a presumably dishonorable man with all the recklessness of which she had accused him. He thought about jumping in the other waiting hackney, just to make sure she got safely home. But the hackney would drop her where she asked, and the biggest danger she would face would be the wrath of her family.

Besides, in some peculiar way, following her would have felt like cheating. He smiled ruefully to himself at this thought as he made his way back to the hotel. She had won the last skirmish in their battles of the evening, and he would not grudge her it.

Back in his room, he took off his coat and cravat and sprawled thoughtfully in the armchair with the unfinished glass of wine. Hers had stained his bed when he had jumped on her, but that was the hotel's problem. It would not disturb his sleep, and he would offer to pay extra for the laundry.

The girl had courage, and she clearly cared for her sister. Was that why she filled his thoughts? Why had he not simply thrown her out of his room and left Renwick's staff to deal with her?

Maybe. Though it didn't explain why he had not gone back to the ball to hunt for entertainment. The wretched girl had distracted him with her mysteries and accusations. And with her delectable, untouched body that she had no idea how to use to best advantage. That had been an unkind test, perhaps, though he could not regret it. It had been a long time since a chaste woman had aroused him.

More to the point, he assured himself, he had seen her face—and it was charming if not quite beautiful in the accepted sense. Her chin was a little too determined, her eyes too frank, her nose just a little too turned up. And an asymmetrical dimple at the corner of her mouth lent her a hint of humor that went well with that wild if luxuriant hair.

If he had met her before, he couldn't recall it. Nor could he conjure up anyone who looked enough like her to be her sister, and presumably he must have at least danced with the sister for his visitor to believe he was the father of the unborn child.

Someone had treated the sister ill. Despite the natural relief any man might feel at discovering he was not responsible for such a situation, he felt bad for the family. And perhaps he owed the sister something for his demonstration on the wine-stained bed. Had he been a younger and more foolish man…

Well, he needn't go there. Everyone was young and foolish at some point, but it was the women who paid the price. Alone. And that was not right. In fact, his visitor would pay the price for her sister's folly, too. Scandal brought down the victim's entire family. Unless it was all hushed up. Which took money and connections. He wondered if they had those.

He finished his wine with a vague idea of finding out who the devil the family was and maybe even making use of his own connections if he had to. Then, although it was ridiculously early by his standards, he prepared for bed.

THERE WAS A certain novel charm in being up with the birds, breakfasted, and driving back into Town at a time before he was normally even awake. Arrived back at Calton House, his Town residence, he shut himself in his library with his correspondence. Unusually, he examined his invitation cards before anything else. There were not so many of those as during the spring Season, but enough people were in London while Parliament sat to make parties worthwhile. Where, he wondered, would he be most likely to run into his enterprising visitor?

Having dashed off a couple of quick acceptance notes, he turned his attention to the weightier business of estate corre-spondence and upcoming parliamentary debates. The vote he cared about most should be done in time for him to get to Lady

Wenning's party at Harcourt before returning to his own estate.

He was deep into his reading on parliamentary reform when James, his butler, informed him that he had visitors.

"Lady Calton, my lord. And Miss Branforth."

Calton groaned. The Dowager Lady Calton was his grandmother, and therefore not to be fobbed off. Which was a pity, for though he was fond of the redoubtable old lady, he knew damned well she had brought along another debutante to persuade him to the altar.

Nevertheless, he put his coat back on and stepped round to the blue salon where he normally received his visitors. There he found his grandmother seated on the sofa beside a pale beauty with downcast eyes, wearing white, sprigged muslin—a very young lady, who appeared to be listening avidly to his grandmother's conversation. Or instruction.

"Grandmama." He crossed the room to take her compellingly outstretched hand, then bent and kissed her cheek. "What an unexpected honor."

"Ha," uttered his grandmother. "You're looking well, Calton. My dear," she added to the young lady, "this graceless scamp is my grandson, the Earl of Calton. Calton, Miss Branforth, Eversleigh's daughter, who has been kind enough to accompany me to the dressmaker's this morning."

The limpid blue eyes raised to his looked curious, also hopeful. He bowed correctly over her hand and murmured welcoming inanities.

"Can I offer you tea, Grandmama?" he said.

"Lord, no, I have to get this child home. I just brought her to meet you because she knows no one in Town as yet. Mourning meant she did not come out in the spring as was originally planned. So, I thought it would be more pleasant for her to recognize at least one face at Lady Darling's ball tonight."

"Sadly, I shall not be at Lady Darling's."

His grandmother's eyes narrowed. "But she told me in particular she had sent you a card."

"Then I sent my apologies." If he had remembered.

"Well, she won't mind. I told her you would be there."

There were times when Calton wondered how it was his grandmother had lived so long. She met his gaze with her own, which contained a wealth of understanding as well as determination. He could win this fight, of course, but why bother? In any case, it was just possible that the girl from Maida would be at the ball.

"You are incorrigible, Grandmama," he observed. "If Lady Darling does not throw me out, I shall be there. And I hope you will save me a dance, Miss Branforth."

"I should enjoy that very much," she said with a grateful smile that irritated him. Why anyone should be grateful to dance with a man clearly only doing his ungracious duty to his grandmother was beyond him.

Because he was an earl, of course.

His grandmother rose to her feet. "Come, then, my dear, let me return you to your mama."

Civilly, Calton accompanied them to the waiting carriage. His grandmother stood back, leaving him to hand Miss Branforth into the carriage first, while the old lady exchanged words with the butler, who had once been her own servant.

"Well, what do you think?" she demanded as soon as Calton sauntered over to the step.

Calton gestured with his eyes and the butler duly backed off inside. "I think she is very pretty, and you are an interfering old woman."

"You'll find she grows on you."

"So do warts."

"Insolent boy. Seriously, you are eight-and-twenty, and the earldom must have an heir."

"Cousin Anthony will make a perfect heir. He even has ten sons to succeed him."

"He has two sons and a daughter, and Anthony was not born to be the earl." She lowered her voice. "Seriously, Calton, you cannot let Francis deflect you from your duty. He has been dead for twelve years."

Calton smiled, to prove the jibe neither hurt nor bothered him. "My dear ma'am, only wickedness deflects me from my duty."

"Hmmph," uttered his grandmother, holding out one commanding hand. "It needn't. Many wicked men are married."

CHAPTER THREE

"WHERE ON EARTH were you?" Helena hissed as soon as their father had departed the breakfast parlor. "I had to cover for you the entire evening, and then you wouldn't speak to me this morning in your bedchamber."

"I was *asleep* this morning in my bedchamber."

"Seriously, Jo, what are you up to? Where did you go?"

Fortunately, they did not have so many servants that any hovered to serve breakfast. Even so, Josephine rose and closed the door before coming back to the table.

"I went to Maida Gardens."

Helena blanched. "With whom?"

"No one. I met Lord Calton there."

Helena closed her eyes. "Dear God. Did you know he was going to be there? Is that why you went?"

"Of course. I heard his servants talking on the area steps when I went to call on him."

"Josephine! You cannot go calling on an unmarried man, who does not even have a mother to play hostess for him!"

"Oh, don't worry, I didn't enter the monster's lair. According to the servants I overheard, he had already gone off to Maida Gardens for a night of debauchery, beginning with the masked ball."

"Please tell me you did not speak to him."

"Why?" Josephine retorted. "Afraid I learned the truth? That you lied to me? That I accused an innocent man?" Not that she believed him to be innocent of very much but being the father of Helena's child seemed to be the one crime he had *not* committed.

Helena sprang to her feet, then held onto the table for support. "You are making everything worse, Jo. By now, there will be rumors all over Town. Why can't you just leave me alone?"

Josephine stared at her. "Because you're not *doing* anything. Are you waiting to be rescued by your handsome prince? You only have me."

"You can't fix it, Jo," Helena whispered. "Not this." And she fled from the room, leaving Josephine with no appetite.

It was more than possible that Helena was right. That in her efforts to make Lord Calton face up to responsibilities that were not—probably—his, she had merely precipitated the moment of Helena's fall. She should have found some way to ensure Calton would keep his mouth shut. Although, of course, he did not know her name, and she was determined to keep it that way.

After her aunt's party tonight, from which, sadly, she could not cry off, she would just have to find ways to avoid society. And when she could not, it should not be too difficult to avoid Lord Calton, for he was both difficult to miss and generally surrounded by friends and beautiful women. He would never even notice her. He certainly never had before. So, he need never know her identity, she thought optimistically.

He noticed me at Maida, she reminded herself ruefully, though only for her novelty, since she had had the temerity to ask him to dance. And it was true he had kissed her on the bed, while…aroused. Well, men were aroused all the time. It meant nothing, and his kiss had been more in the nature of a lesson that she could easily hate him for.

Except that now she knew what a real kiss felt like. And it was rather wonderful.

Frowning as she nibbled half-heartedly on a piece of toast, she wondered if the kiss was why she imagined he was too honorable to tell tales. No doubt Helena had thought the same thing of her errant swain.

Her Aunt Darling—or Darling Aunt as Josephine and Helena had always called her—drifted into the room in a cloud of diaphanous shawls. "Oh, good, Josephine!" She beamed. "Come and tell me what you think of the ballroom. Since you have danced all over Europe, you will have excellent taste."

"I'm not sure the two necessarily go together," Josephine murmured, "but I would love to see it."

After she had duly admired the potted palms and swathes of decorative silk and heard all about the hothouse roses that would be delivered en masse late this afternoon, it struck her that she could do worse than pick her aunt's brains.

"I suppose everyone who is anyone will be coming tonight," she said.

"Well, everyone who is in Town. It won't be the shocking squeeze one hopes for in the Season." She rattled off several names, all of which passed over Josephine's head, though she gathered they were leaders of London society.

In truth, Josephine knew very few people in Town. They had only come home to England from Paris in June and gone straight to their grandmother's house in Bath. From there, they had gone to stay with Lady Darling, Papa's widowed sister, in Brighton and only returned with her to London because Josephine's father, a respected diplomat, had been summoned by the Foreign Secretary.

"What of Lord Calton?" she asked casually. "We met him in Brighton. He danced with Helena."

Aunt Darling waved one dismissive hand. "Oh, he won't come. Old Lady Calton told me he would, but that's wishful thinking. He sent me his apologies weeks ago. I think he's off to the continent. Or will be soon. He's the despair of the matchmaking mamas—and grandmamas!"

His absence was not quite the relief she had imagined it would be. Which was odd because it certainly meant one less thing to worry about.

When she was dressed for the ball that evening, she went in search of Helena, whom she found anxiously smoothing her gown over her stomach.

"There is nothing to see," Josephine assured her, leaning against the closed door. "But I would not examine yourself like that too often around the maids."

Helena grimaced. "I won't need to in another few weeks because it will be obvious."

"Calton is not coming," Josephine told her. "According to Aunt. And even if he were, he does not know who I am. You have danced with him, talked to him. Do you think he is a decent man?"

"He is an amusing man, happy to flirt or be friends, though only on a superficial level. I doubt anyone knows him."

Josephine blinked. "Well, you discovered that much."

"I thought about him. After you told me what you did last night." Their eyes met in the glass. "I know you were trying to help me, Jo, and I do thank you for it. But please promise me you won't take any more risks? God knows what could have happened to you at that place, and it would help neither of us for *you* to be…in any kind of trouble." She turned away from the glass to face her. "Calton *was*…kind to you, wasn't he?"

She felt herself flushing. "In his way. Though I am in no hurry to meet him again. Come, we had best go down or Aunt will send a search party for us."

Aunt Darling was their father's sister, and since she was a widow, he played host for the evening. As a result, Josephine discovered several of the guests were her father's fellow diplomats. Sir Joseph and Lady Sayle were among the first to arrive, followed by Prince and Princess Esterhazy, thus ensuring the success of Darling Aunt's party. For Josephine, it was very pleasant to find such old friends here, especially, perhaps, Andre de Talley, whom they had first met in Vienna as part of the French delegation to the peace congress. He had been a particular friend over the years, hungry enough to do difficult work well for his defeated country, and young enough to enjoy himself when opportunity offered.

"What a pleasant surprise!" Josephine greeted him, offering both her hands. "We did not even know you were in London!"

"I have been here since the summer. But I ran into Mr. Blackwell last week and he invited me, so here I am. And you look ravishing as always! But where is… Ah."

Helena was already on the arm of someone Josephine didn't recognize, strolling toward the dance floor.

"I must wait until later so speak to Miss Blackwell," Talley observed. "But you will dance with me, Miss Jo?"

"I would be delighted," Josephine agreed, relieved to have so amiable a partner, for the gift of easy conversation cultivated by diplomatic families seemed to have largely passed her by. Talley, however, had taken her and Helena riding in the Vienna Woods and mischief-making at several masked balls. So that whenever they had run into each other across Europe, she had been glad.

"So, will your posting to London be a long one?" she asked as the opening waltz began.

"Perhaps. Mr. Blackwell tells me he will be here for the fore-seeable future. Are you pleased?"

Josephine wrinkled her nose. "It all seems very staid, to be honest, though it is good to be with my aunt, who is very tolerant of us all."

"Perhaps you and Miss Blackwell will ride with me in the park one morning?"

"We would love to," Josephine said without hesitation before she remembered her sister's condition. Helena was not at her best in the early mornings. And then she remembered another waltz with another man and her insides tightened all over again. *Well, at least he is not here.*

And that was when, just as if she had conjured him from her thoughts, she saw him over Talley's shoulder, sauntering into the ballroom.

Her heart performed a violent somersault, and she immediately jerked her gaze away. But somehow, his image seemed to be printed on her eyelids, for she could still see him overlaying the man she danced with.

Despite the very different surroundings, in perfect evening dress, Lord Calton contrived somehow to look just as jaded and dashing as last night. And, of course, just as spectacularly handsome.

"Josephine?" Talley's concerned voice broke into her shock. "Are you quite well?"

"Mmm? Oh. Yes, of course." She smiled at him. "I beg your pardon—a sudden slip of memory. How do you like living in London?"

⇛⇚

CALTON HAD SEEN her almost as soon as he had entered the ballroom, waltzing with the same grace she had shown last night, but laughing up at her partner in an open way she never had with him. Gone was the mysterious seductress and in her place a friendly and probably charming young woman.

Two sides of the same coin. He didn't doubt there were others. But who the devil was she?

Lady Darling was a goddaughter of his grandmother's, so the old lady, sitting with her cronies among the dowagers, was a good place to begin. He made his way toward her, pausing to greet old friends and acquaintances en route.

"Dear me, can it possibly be Lord Calton himself?" drawled an amused voice he knew only too well. "I thought your lordship had quite given us up for the blandishments of Paris."

Calton kept the faint smile on his lips as he turned toward the lady who had been, up until last week, his mistress. Mrs. Selina Reddington was lovely, languid, and not without thorns. He was well aware of the barbs in her greeting, since his upcoming trip to the continent had been the main reason he had given her for their parting.

In fact, his journey had been an excuse, for in truth, he was as bored with her as with the rest of his life. He could not help believing there should be more attraction to one's lover than experience in the bedchamber and a complaisant husband, which were the only qualities she had exhibited or that he had chosen to see. They were not good for each other. He had told her that, too, though he had the feeling the remark had gone straight over her head.

He took her elegantly offered hand and bowed over it. "Your servant, Mrs. Reddington. As you see, arrangements are taking longer than I expected." He glanced at her companion, whom he did not know—a young, handsome man, who looked quite the Corinthian with his short hair and severely smart style. And a wary expression. Did he imagine Calton was here to reclaim Selina?

"Are you gentlemen not acquainted?" Selina asked in apparent surprise. "Calton, allow me to present Mr. Gough, Lord Denzil's heir. George, my old friend, the Earl of Calton."

By which, Calton realized, faintly amused, that they were both supposed to recognize that Gough was his replacement in her bed. Perhaps there was something wrong with Calton that he should care so little. God, he needed to get away from Town, from the sordid little pleasures that had somehow become his life.

He and the Corinthian sprig exchanged slight bows, and Calton excused himself with the bizarre feeling that he needed to brush off his hands.

The waltz was coming to an end, so he put on a burst of speed to reach his grandmother before it did.

"Ah, Calton, so you did make the time," the old lady greeted him, breaking off her involved conversation to offer him her hand and her cheek, both of which he saluted dutifully.

"As commanded, though Lady Darling looked utterly confused to see me."

"The Branforth chit is over there," his grandmother nodded across the room, "by the smaller palm."

"I shall bear it in mind," he assured her. "Satisfy my curiosity about another young lady. The one in green, with the dark-haired fellow."

As the dance came to a final close, the lady in question curtsied to her partner and took his arm, immediately and annoyingly turning her back to Calton. He wondered if she had seen him and if it was deliberate.

"He's French," his grandmother said dismissively. "Related to Talleyrand, you know—though he's shortened his name for some reason—so at least he is a gentleman. No idea who the girl is."

"Good Lord," Calton said, not entirely joking. "How can this be?"

"Either she's new in Town or she's a nobody," his grandmother replied airily. "Well, go on, you've done your duty by me. Now go away and enjoy yourself."

"Perhaps, I shall," Calton murmured, and with a bow, strolled off in pursuit of the unknown girl.

It didn't take him long to realize that she was deliberately avoiding him, flitting around the ballroom from her dance partner to a group of young ladies, to Lady Darling's brother and host for the evening, and to another dance partner for the country dance. Unless he was prepared to stride across the room and plant himself right in front of her, she was likely to remain at least one step ahead of him for the entire evening.

Accordingly, he switched tactics, and after making brief conversation with Miss Branforth and her gratified mama, asked the younger lady to dance. Unfortunately, they could not join the same set as his quarry, but he caught sight of her occasionally, enough to know she was not quite so comfortable with her current dancing partner as the last, though she still appeared friendly and unselfconsciously graceful.

Of course, he was never so rude as to ignore his own partner, who smiled at him frequently and chattered whenever the dance brought them together. Only once did he catch an expression in her eyes that looked very like triumph.

It wasn't so surprising. For a debutante, who was not of his family or related to a close friend, to dance with the Earl of Calton was at least a rarity. His gift of social cachet, he thought sardonically. He didn't blame her precisely—she was little more than a child, after all, encouraged by her parents, to say nothing of his own grandmother—but he could not help his twinge of distaste. He was fed up being regarded as a prize.

Really, just as soon as he had solved the mystery of last night's visitor, it was time for pastures new. Returning Miss Branforth to her preening mama, he made his escape and began prowling the ballroom once more. This time, he made no effort to pursue his quarry. Instead, he hunted her first dancing partner and was soon fortunate enough to come upon the man with someone he knew.

"Dearham!" Calton thrust out his hand with genuine pleasure. "I didn't know you were in Town."

"Doing my parliamentary duty," the Duke of Dearham said with one of his infectious grins as they shook hands. "How are you? I heard you were off to Paris."

"Arranging it," Calton said easily, letting his gaze flit over Dearham's companion.

"Do you know Monsieur de Talley?" Dearham said. "On the French Ambassador's staff. Monsieur, my good friend, the Earl of Calton."

Calton offered his hand and had it civilly if firmly shaken. "How fortunate to meet you. You must give me a native's perspective on the best places to visit in your country."

"You will make a long stay?" Talley asked.

"Possibly. I mean to follow my nose from Calais and see where it takes me. Can I interest you gentlemen in a game of cards?"

"Perhaps later," Dearham said. "I am committed to proving that it is not unfashionable to dance with one's own wife. If you will excuse me…"

"Monsieur de Talley?"

"Why not?" The Frenchman began to walk beside him.

"Talking of dancing," Calton said, watching as Dearham led his wife onto the floor, "who was the young lady I saw you waltz with earlier? I was sure I knew her, but name and context elude me."

"Miss Josephine Blackwell? She is Lady Darling's niece."

Calton blinked. "Is she, by God? How can my grandmother not have known that? Does she have a sister, by chance?"

"Miss Blackwell is stepping onto the floor with Sir Joseph Sayle."

He followed the Frenchman's gaze and did indeed recall the elder Miss Blackwell from an early summer jaunt to Brighton. He had solved the mystery, though he felt no desire to smile. "Ah, that explains it," he murmured as they entered the card room. "I have danced with Miss Blackwell and never met the younger sister after all. Piquet?"

CHAPTER FOUR

JOSEPHINE DID NOT dare to go near her sister until Calton disappeared into the card room. Unfortunately, he was in the company of Talley, who would be able to tell him anything he asked.

She rather rushed her tolerant partner into the same set as Helena and stood beside her sister. "He's here," she murmured.

"I know. It's fine." Helena sounded distracted rather than worried, and as far as Josephine could tell, no one was yet looking at them askance.

By the end of the dance, Calton and Talley had emerged from the card room once more. Calton was leaning against the wall as they made apparently amusing conversation together, but the attention of both men seemed to be focused on her. Or on Helena.

"I'll keep out of your way," Josephine muttered and all but bolted across the room to her father's side. He looked somewhat surprised to see her but happily introduced her to the serious older gentlemen he'd been conversing with. The serious older gentlemen seemed charmed.

Her nerves skittered when she saw Calton approach Helena. But to her surprise, he said something that made her sister smile and accept his hand for the next dance. A sense of foreboding came over Josephine. She even shivered as though, as Nurse had put it, someone had walked over her grave.

"Forgive me, ma'am, but I think you dropped this?"

Josephine blinked. A stranger stood in front of her, blocking her view of Helena and Lord Calton, offering her a wisp of embroidered lawn.

"Oh, how foolish," she managed, reaching out to take the handkerchief. Then she paused and frowned. "Actually, that is not mine. I am glad to say the folly was someone else's."

"Mine," the stranger admitted with a rueful smile that invited her to share the joke. "I hoped you would not notice, but the truth is I have been looking for an excuse to speak to you and no one has introduced us."

"Why do you want to speak to me?" she asked curiously as the handkerchief vanished into his pocket. "Do you keep a lady's handkerchief in your pocket just in case you wish to accost someone?"

"I want to ask you to dance. And of course not. I found it by my chair this evening and could not find its owner. So will you honor me with the dance?"

Josephine hesitated. Although it was not quite proper to dance with strangers, she had never seen the harm in a room positively awash with chaperones. And since he was here at all, he was clearly known to her aunt. Besides, on the dance floor, she would be nearer to Helena in the event of her sister needing her for any reason.

And then, she realized now that she looked properly, the man was good-looking, with a twinkle of mischief in his eyes.

"I will, if you tell me your name," she said.

He bowed. "The Honorable Cyril Gough, at your service. And you, I think, are Miss Blackwell."

She laid her fingertips on his proffered arm. "I am. Although Miss Blackwell is more properly my elder sister. I am Miss Josephine Blackwell."

"How charming. Were you named for the late empress?"

"My father has always denied it." She allowed him to turn her and take her hand, circling her waist with his arm. Beyond him, she could see Helena, who looked slightly flushed but not unhappy.

The waltz began.

"I gather you traveled all over Europe with your father," Mr. Gough said.

"And beyond."

"Then you must have had an unusually varied upbringing for a young lady."

"I suppose we did, but since I knew nothing else, I accepted it. We were well looked after, you know," she added with amusement. "My father did not abandon us alone in the jungle!"

"Of course, he did not. I am merely intrigued by the views of such a well-traveled lady. And perhaps a little jealous. Did you meet Lord Calton abroad?"

She blinked. "No." Then, remembering her part, "I don't believe I have met him at all."

"Oh, I thought I saw you looking at him when I first approached you. I thought he might have made you unhappy."

"Acquit him, sir," she said lightly. "It was my sister I was watching. She was feeling a little under the weather earlier today, and I was worried for her."

"You are a careful sister. And yet she is the elder."

"We have always looked after each other."

"Well, I am glad to hear it. Not that I wish ill health upon Miss Blackwell, you understand! But I would worry considerably more were you smitten with Lord Calton."

"You would have no right," she pointed out. "And you certainly have no reason."

"None beyond the fact that he is the kind of aristocrat I most dislike—entitled, wasteful, and careless of the feelings of lesser mortals."

Annoyingly, she had to stop herself from leaping to Calton's defense, which was odd to say the least. "Are you not also from a titled family?" she asked innocently. In fact, he had made sure she knew it by introducing himself as *the Honorable* Mr. Gough, which was hardly usual.

"Heir to a mere barony," he said dismissively.

"Mere? I am sure it comes with many responsibilities."

"It does, but why are we discussing me? I had much rather talk about you?"

"Why?"

He laughed. "*That* is why! That and your quite unusual beauty."

Which was, she knew, another way of saying she didn't have any beauty at all. Helena had all the looks of the family, which was fine by Josephine, though it annoyed her slightly when people tried to console her by saying things like "unusual beauty," as though physical appearance was the only reason to be alive, let alone admired.

CALTON RATHER LIKED Helena Blackwell. In fact, he remembered rather liking her the last time they had danced, several weeks previously, although the feeling had been vague and easily forgotten. Now, as they danced and walked and went into supper together, he wondered how to bring the conversation discreetly around to her problems, all without being overheard.

It was she who pushed aside her barely touched supper and said, "I believe I would like a little fresh air before returning to the ballroom."

"Allow me to escort you," Calton offered, rising. "In fact, let me bring a plate and we can continue al fresco on the terrace."

They were not the only people on the terrace, but a small table set between two cushioned benches at one end was secluded enough for private conversation while still being easily seen by everyone else.

"The autumn evenings are chilly," Calton said, handing her

onto one of the benches and placing the plate on the table. "Shall I fetch a shawl?"

"Oh, no, I won't stay long enough to notice," she said with something of her sister's unflattering honesty. "I just wanted to say something to you."

He sat opposite her. "Say on."

She eyed him with a mixture of wariness and conscious courage. "I understand you met my sister last night. Where she had no business to be."

"I don't recall it."

She smiled. "Yes, you do, but thank you for saying so. I don't want you to think badly of her. She was only trying to help me and never thinks how her actions might be misconstrued."

"I understand."

"I think you probably do," she said ruefully, "which makes it even more strange that you are sitting here rather than cutting me dead."

He didn't pretend to misunderstand her. "It takes two, Miss Blackwell, and it is not fair that women must pay the price."

"That is true. Neither is it fair that it was your name I gave my sister, just to make her leave me alone. I should have known she wouldn't leave *you* alone. My only excuse is that my mind is…preoccupied. But I hope you will accept my apology."

"There is no need," Calton said. "I would rather know how I might help you."

She frowned at him. "You should be running from me. Aren't you afraid I will try to trick you into an offer of marriage?"

"By compromising me on the terrace?" he asked, fluttering his eyelashes.

It drew a short laugh from her. "Don't worry, I shan't be so stupid or so ill-bred. In any case, I thank you for the offer of help, but there is nothing you can do."

"There might be. If I knew who it was I should speak to."

"No," she said in quick alarm. "I will not have him—" She broke off, biting her lip and staring at her food.

"Inconvenienced?" Calton said in disbelief, and when she flushed, he pressed home his point. "My dear girl, you will be ruined, and if you choose that over a point of pride, it is, of course, your decision. But your sister will fall with you. And your father's career is likely to suffer, too."

She closed her eyes. "I know that. And I will do my very best not to let it happen. I just cannot quite see my way."

"If a quiet word—or a thrashing—would help, I am your man."

Her eyes flew open again. "I would not have you think ill of him. He is a good and honorable man, and I cannot press him into a marriage he is not prepared for."

That he should have been prepared the moment he touched her went without saying. Especially as another realization hit Calton with force. "He doesn't know."

Her eyes fell again, and she shook her head.

Calton leaned forward. "He needs to know. You are worrying yourself sick like this. And that is not good for the child *or* you."

"How do you know about such matters?" she retorted. "Do you have many children of your own?"

"No. But I am responsible for a lot of people."

She regarded him with some curiosity. "You are not at all what I expected."

"Like everyone else, I have my good moments along with the bad." Some movement beyond her shoulder caught his attention. Josephine Blackwell leaned out of the French doors to the ballroom, caught sight of them, and whisked herself inside again. Calton's lips twitched as he returned his gaze to the elder Miss Blackwell. "If you won't let me help you, please speak to *him*."

She seemed to think about that. "If you would really like to help me, and the worst comes to the worst, will you do your best for Jo? Despite everything, I think she trusts you. Likes you, even." She rose to her feet. "I shall go and find my aunt. Thank you for your kindness, my lord."

And she walked away, leaving him gazing thoughtfully at the

slightly less-full plate. Taking a small pastry, he swung his leg over the back of the bench and gazed out over the small garden to the mews beyond.

"I think she trusts you. Likes you, even." A smile began to play around his lips. He had no reason to hope it was true, and yet he did.

JOSEPHINE HAD SPENT the first hour of the ball avoiding Lord Calton. He then appeared to lose interest and ignore her, but along with the relief of that had come fresh anxiety. What was he saying to Helena? Was he flirting with her? Making horrible assumptions because of Josephine's idiocy last night?

She had been appalled to see them leave the supper room together, and, when she casually followed, to discover them tete-a-tete on the terrace. Not that this was compromising in any way. Another couple at the near end of the terrace had the same idea, and several people strolled between. But still…

As she jerked herself back inside, hopefully before either Calton or Helena noticed her, she was conscious of an unpleasant little twist of emotion that she could not identify. Something worse than anxiety and impatience, something to do with the comfortable intensity of their talk. Unwilling to examine it, she merely made a brief visit to the ladies' cloakroom and then hurried back to the terrace.

Whether from the chill or because the supper hour was all but over, people were beginning to drift back inside. Lord Calton was still there, though she could not see Helena.

Did the terrace wrap around the other side of the ballroom, too? She could not remember ever looking. Was Calton just waiting there until everyone else was back inside to…

To what? she asked herself fiercely. *Compromise Helena? Take advantage?* She might imagine him to be honorable enough to keep her secrets, but she did not know him. And since he seemed to be deep in thought and facing the other direction, she flitted down the length of the terrace to find only a narrow vegetable patch between the end of it and the kitchen door. And, of course, there was no sign of Helena or anyone else there.

She began to creep back the way she had come.

"You *could* just speak to me," Calton said without turning.

"Why would I do that?"

"I could tell you that Miss Blackwell went back inside a few minutes ago and is probably with Lady Darling."

"Thank you," she said stiffly. Then, "How did you know it was me?"

"Your perfume."

She scowled at his back. "I don't *wear* perfume."

"Then your body smells naturally delightful."

"You," she said crossly, walking toward him without meaning to, "are trying to provoke me."

He rose and turned to face her, and she paused mid-stride. Somehow, she had forgotten how large he was, and even in the poor light, the fresh realization caught at her breath. Or something did.

She sat down on the bench her sister had previously occupied, and he lowered himself back to his own, facing her this time. The lantern light coming mostly from the low terrace wall cast shadows along the sharp lines of his cheekbones and made his eyes glint, though whether with humor or something more sinister remained to be seen.

"Your sister is very proud and very stubborn," he observed.

Josephine nodded. "I should have known she had not given in and told me. For whatever it is worth, I'm sorry."

"Don't be. I was charmed to meet you."

She actually laughed, a short, breathless sound. "Liar. I spoiled your evening." And then, before she could bite her tongue, "Why did you kiss me?"

He was silent. Then he said, "To teach you a lesson? Or because I was angry at being so easily bested?"

She nodded. "That is what I thought."

"Mostly," he added, "I kissed you because I wanted to. The more interesting question is why you kissed me back."

"I did not!" Her cheeks burned. Everything burned. "You took me by surprise."

"That is true also. Next time, I shall give you plenty of warning."

She jumped to her feet. "There will not be a next time, sir," she said with dignity. "It may be my fault—well, it *is* my fault— but you have entirely the wrong idea about my sister and me. Good evening."

She turned on her heel and stalked off, though she had not taken more than a step before she found him beside her. His ungloved fingers closed around her gloved ones and placed them on his arm, holding them there for a moment when she would have pulled free.

"Don't get in a miff," he murmured. "I'm only flirting."

"I do not *flirt*," she said dangerously.

"You managed well enough last night."

"That was to get your attention," she muttered.

"Well, you succeeded."

Her gaze flew up to his in astonishment, because just for a moment, she thought he meant more than last night, that she *still* had his attention, and that idea was somehow overwhelming, intoxicating.

And there were too many people around to ask for clarification, supposing she had the nerve.

His eyes smiled beguilingly down at her. One even fluttered closed so quickly, she could never be sure whether or not he actually *winked*.

"There you are, Jo," Aunt Darling said, rustling up to them. "I believe you are promised to Mr. Campbell for this dance."

Lord Calton relinquished her hand with a bow and with another to Lady Darling, he strolled off, leaving her feeling curiously dazed.

FLIRTING WITH JOSEPHINE Blackwell was unexpectedly fun, although even as he gave in to the inclination, he was aware that he was more than teasing. Whether for the sake of his pathetic male pride or just because she amused him, *he* wanted *her* attention. He had been right at Maida. She was different, though he couldn't quite put his finger on how or why. Nor did he wish to look into the matter too closely. In a few days, he would leave London, either for the continent or for the Wennings' party, en route to the continent. Although he would like things to be more settled for Helena Blackwell before that.

He had no reason to feel responsible for Helena's condition, but he could not help the odd notion that Josephine had somehow *made* him so. He drew the line at marrying Helena himself—that would be disastrous for all concerned—but he did want to see her happily established. And so, he made a point of speaking to her again before the end of the ball.

He chose a moment when her father was in earshot, as well as Lady Darling, to be sure everything was seen to be above board and without scandal.

"We talked about riding in the park one morning, Miss Blackwell. Perhaps you are free the day after tomorrow?"

His aim was to have another opportunity to talk to her, to make her see the reality of her choices going forward, but it had an unexpected benefit that he almost missed.

One of the gentlemen on the fringe of her group jerked his head around. It was only a moment, but the glare in his eyes could have annihilated Bonaparte's Old Guard. And then, almost before Calton had registered it, he turned back to Sir Joseph Sayle with whom he was in conversation.

Well, Monsieur de Talley. That is interesting.

CHAPTER FIVE

"HE INVITED YOU to go riding?" Josephine said cautiously to her sister the following day. They were seated in the morning room with Aunt Darling, who was dealing with her correspondence while the sisters worked on their embroidery. Well, Helena worked. Josephine mostly stared at hers and thought of other things.

Now, however, she gazed, frowning, at Helena. She had the horrible feeling she recognized the unpleasant twinge in her heart, which felt like the one that had assailed her at the sight of Lord Calton and Helena together on the terrace. But she must be wrong. She could not be jealous of her own sister, and certainly not over *Calton*.

"Tomorrow morning," Helena said. "But it is quite proper. He suggested making a party of it. Do you know, I think Lord Calton's reputation probably lies?"

"It doesn't," Aunt Darling said from her desk. "But I never heard that he deflowered innocent girls of good family beneath the noses of their fathers. You will be perfectly safe. For the record, he is also very wealthy, his title is old, and he would make an excellent match. Of course, you will go." She glanced up. "Both of you, with Fredericks."

"Why is he not married already?" Helena asked.

Aunt Darling shrugged. "Too interested in his own pleasures, though old Lady Calton implies there is more to it than that. Which is what gives me hope that he might settle down if he chose one—"

"What more?" Josephine asked before she could help herself.

"He had a brother who died at the age of twelve or so." Aunt Darling looked uncomfortable. "This is not for gossip, just between us. The boy was…different. Looked odd and didn't grow intellectually as a child should. Calton was very cut-up when he died, and Lady Calton believes he is afraid of siring a child like his brother."

"Because it would embarrass him to have such an heir," Helena mused.

"Because he would see his child die," Josephine said slowly, then, discovering both pairs of eyes on her, she hastily concentrated on her needlework and changed the subject. But however much truth there was in her aunt's or her own speculations, the story deepened her view of him as someone who cared deeply, however badly he behaved. She could even imagine him avoiding caring by relentless pleasure-seeking. Up to a point, although many experiences formed every character.

She forced herself to consider him in relation to her sister's problem. Marriage to Lord Calton would, she thought cautiously, be the perfect solution for Helena. He knew the truth and would treat her with respect. And he would, besides, be easy to fall in love with.

So why didn't she like the idea?

Because he would not be faithful. Or perhaps he would. After all, surely Helena was easy to fall in love with, too? He would have to love her a great deal, for her child would become his heir. And not being of his blood might even be a good thing, from his point of view…

Well, she could not plan for this, she could only watch and help if possible.

So, it was with a sense of excitement, and yet an inexplicable knot in the pit of her stomach, that she set off for Hyde Park the next day, mounted on her old friend, Silver, and accompanied by Helena and Fredericks, their father's groom.

It was early enough for both streets and park to be quiet, which was fortunate, for Silver was in a frisky mood and clearly wanted to stretch her legs. She kept sidling about, trying to nudge Helena's Gold and entice her, no doubt, to equally bad behavior.

Waiting for them just inside the Cumberland Gate was Lord Calton, looking casually splendid on a shining black giant of a horse. And emerging from behind him on a chestnut almost as large, Andre de Talley.

"Talley! We didn't expect to see you, too," Josephine exclaimed, which neatly left Calton to greet Helena first and allowed Josephine to meet him afterward with mere, off-hand friendliness. Though why something as simple as a mere greeting should be so difficult, she had no idea.

"You and his lordship have become friends?" she asked Talley lightly as they set off up the main path behind Helena and Calton.

Talley shrugged. "Hardly that, though he is amiable and amusing. When he heard I had no mount in England, he offered me the use of one of his, beginning with this morning's outing. Tell me, is your sister quite well?"

"She is a little under the weather," Josephine replied. "But not ill."

"I wondered because she does not look quite her usual ebullient self. And at the ball, I was afraid she was avoiding me."

"I'm sure she was not," Josephine said awkwardly. More likely, Helena did not want old friends who knew her well remarking on the changes within her. Even their father had noticed she was looking a little peaky, and Aunt Darling kept trying to tempt her appetite. Silver sidled again, tugging insistently on the reins, and Josephine raised her voice so that the two in front could hear also, "Shall we find somewhere quieter to let them gallop? Silver won't behave until she does."

Lord Calton led the way off the main drive and across the park to a more open space. With relief—her hands were getting tired keeping the mare in check—Josephine gave Silver her head and they sped off across the grass. With the rush of the wind in her face and the joy of the gallop, she let go of her anxieties, just for a moment, and enjoyed the exhilaration of the ride.

Even when Lord Calton drew alongside her, she only smiled at him. And when he smiled back with what could only be a shared love of speed, the rest of the world receded into the pleasure of the moment.

Of course, it could only be a moment, for it was not proper for ladies to gallop in the park. She slowed Silver as another path and some people came into view and petted her neck as they came to a standstill.

"She is a fine animal," Calton said, pulling up beside her. "And you ride very well."

"For a woman?" she challenged.

"For anyone. But I fear we have left the others behind."

"Talley will look after Helena. And Fredericks, of course."

A humorous, half-flirting look entered his eyes.

Don't dare ask who will look after me…

He said, "I gather Monsieur de Talley is an old friend."

"Yes, we met in Vienna, during the Congress, and since then seem to keep running into each other. He even turned up in Brighton when we stayed there with my aunt. He was delivering something to the Prince Regent, I believe. And now he seems settled in London."

"You like him?"

She frowned at him. "We all like him. Including my father. Why?"

"Ask me again later. Tell me, has your sister considered all the possibilities of her situation?"

"To be honest, she seems to be merely panicking and considering nothing very much at all. Which is why I felt obliged to step in, though, of course, I made it worse."

"No, you didn't. If we need to, I can arrange for her—with you, if you wish it—to stay abroad for a time and have the child adopted. There could be an invitation from a cousin of mine in Tuscany or another in Switzerland, a chance to improve Miss Blackwell's health in sun or mountain air."

She tore her gaze free, staring at Silver's ears. "Thank you," she managed, then, "Why are you doing this for us?"

He said nothing until she glanced at him. His lips quirked upward. "You asked for my help."

"No, I didn't. I held you up at gunpoint with false accusations and disastrous commands. I thought she must love you."

"Do you think she still loves the father of her child?"

Josephine nodded, feeling an inconvenient lump in her throat. "She is loyal, and her feelings are deep."

"Then she was not…taken advantage of?"

"You mean forced?" Josephine asked bluntly. "I don't believe so. I saw no signs of distress until…she suspected her condition. On the contrary, she was happy to be home in England, enjoyed the gaiety of Brighton. And, you know, my father did not bring us up in complete ignorance."

He nodded. Helena and Talley came into view, their horses walking together in apparent harmony.

"She doesn't gallop anymore," Josephine said sadly.

"She will again."

Galloping hooves from the other direction had them turning to face a solitary rider. He seemed to be about to pass them by at some distance, but then changed direction and came toward them, slowing to a walk.

Although he looked familiar, it took Josephine a moment to place him.

"Mr. Gough," Calton said, "good morning."

"My lord. Miss Josephine. A beautiful autumnal morning for a ride, is it not?"

Gough, of course. She had danced with him, and he had warned her about entitled aristocrats like Lord Calton.

"I never took you for an early riser, my lord," Gough added with a smile.

Calton raised one aristocratic eyebrow. "I would be surprised if you took me for anything at all."

Gough laughed and waved to the approaching Talley and Helena. They rode on all together at a more sedate pace. Calton, after his possible set-down, appeared to accept Gough's presence and even made conversation that kept the man beside him and Josephine. It crossed Josephine's mind that Calton was somehow protecting Helena by doing so, for she had the feeling he did not care for Mr. Gough.

"Where do you stable your horses?" Calton asked him as they approached the park gate once more.

"Oh, over at the livery stable by St. Paul's. It has changed hands recently—I believe one of the Gorses took it over—and it suits me well enough while I have rooms."

Calton nodded. "Then since we go in a different direction, we'll bid you good morning here."

It was almost a dismissal, and Mr. Gough clearly felt it as such for he flushed but could only bow and murmur farewells before heading eastward and leaving Calton, as it were, in possession of the field.

"You don't like him," Josephine observed.

"Do you?"

"I scarcely know him."

Calton said no more on the subject. For the rest of the short distance back to Aunt Darling's house, they rode in a group, indulging in amiable banter, which even Helena joined in.

At the front door, before it was even opened, Calton dismounted and to Josephine's surprise, turned immediately to help her. She hesitated, frowning, for although she couldn't say so, it was really Helena who needed help. But there was Talley, also dismounting to help, leaving Fredericks with nothing to do.

While Josephine observed, Calton merely grasped her by the waist and lifted her to the ground. For an instant, she could not move. Surprise seemed to have paralyzed her. Or perhaps it was the same awareness of his nearness, of the remembered heat and scent of his body that deprived her of breath.

She could not step away because of Silver at her back. A flush spread from his firm hands through her whole body. One could drown in those fascinating blue eyes. One could want to.

His hands slid away, and he stepped back, tipping his hat. "Miss Josephine."

She hurried up the steps, mostly because Helena took her arm. She did not actually stumble, though, at the front door, she turned and looked back over her shoulder. Calton swung up into the saddle with easy grace, saying something to Talley that made the Frenchman smile.

Then the door closed behind her, and she wondered what on earth had just happened.

CALTON KNEW WHAT had happened. In his room at Renwick's Hotel, he had deliberately made her aware of her own desires and his. And now she was remembering. It was a complication he did not need in his life, so why her confused wonder should please him, he had no idea. Not that it meant anything. Desires came and went as he knew only too well. So, he kept his mind on the main problem he had taken it upon himself to solve.

"Has Miss Josephine always been so much livelier than her sister?" he asked Andre de Talley.

Tally frowned. "No. To be honest, I am worried about Miss Blackwell's health. Josephine used to be in her shadow, and now it seems to be the other way around."

"I think you cheered her a little."

A rueful smile flickered across Talley's lips. "Do you think so? Something—" He broke off, shaking his head and cursing under his breath in French.

"Did you talk to her about her health?" Calton asked innocently.

"No, not after the usual courtesies. One cannot tell a lady she is losing her looks."

"One certainly does not need to put it like that."

Talley glared. "It is not even true. Her beauty merely grows…wraith-like."

Calton remained silent, but it seemed the Frenchman was not yet ready to confide, and intrusive questions would only alienate him at this point. So, he changed the subject. "Feel free to borrow the horse whenever you wish."

"Thank you, you are very kind. Tell me about this Gough fellow."

"A friend of the family," Calton said casually, "should probably warn Lady Darling or Mr. Blackwell if he continues to sniff around them. But I suppose they will be off to join the Wennings' party next week."

"I suppose they will," Talley said gloomily.

"You have not been invited? Being in diplomatic circles, I assumed you would know the Wennings well."

"I do know them. But my particular diplomatic circle is the one that does the work. In short, I do not have leave."

"Ah." Calton changed the subject again and made a mental note to interfere with Talley's superiors.

THE HONORABLE MR. Cyril Gough was shown into Mrs. Reddington's private sitting room without a quibble. She sat in a comfortable chair, wrapped in a voluminous silk robe while her maid polished her nails. At sight of him, her hand curled, hiding her nails from the maid, whom she dismissed with a bored wave of the same hand.

"Cyril," she drawled. "What brings you back to me so soon?"

"Soon? It has been more than a day, my love."

"Has it? I did not notice. But my question stands, since I'm not sure I care to be sought in private without prior invitation."

He threw himself into the chair opposite. "I encountered your old amour in the park, and he contrived to annoy me."

She glanced up from admiring her nails. "Did he indeed? Because of me?"

"Because of arrogance and self-importance. I found him in company with the Blackwell sisters."

"Lady Darling's little protegees?" she asked, amused. "Eccentric nobodies. They will never take in London, whatever fuss was made of them in foreign towns."

"That may be so, but Calton looked pretty—er…taken."

That got her attention. Which was both gratifying and annoying. No man likes his mistress to pay quite so much attention to her previous protector.

"Did he, indeed?" she murmured. A flash of annoyance might have shown in her eyes before amusement swept it away. "My dear Cyril, Calton has no possible interest in some ingenue, passing or otherwise!"

"You call them ingenues," Gough said irritably, "but these innocents have danced with kings and emperors in foreign capitals, traveled across Europe and, no doubt, had greater problems to solve than whether to wear the same evening gown twice in a month. There is more to sophistication than bed sport."

A frown flickered on her brow. Something very like venom spat from her eyes before her lashes swept down. "You know, I believe you are right, Cyril? In either case, I am finding you rather less sophisticated than I had hoped. Unless you are prepared to improve your conversation, I believe I can dispense with your company."

She did not say whether she meant for the morning or for good, but it was enough to remind Gough of his manners.

"I am thinking of ways to punish Calton for his poor choices," he told her smoothly. "And for his arrogance."

"And how do you propose to do that?" she asked in clear amusement.

"Did I not hear that the Blackwell sisters are heiresses?"

She shrugged. "Up to a point. They are to inherit the Darling fortune when their aunt dies. Which is not huge but not negligible either. Calton has no need to marry money."

"Nor do I," Gough said swiftly, "though I'll not deny a little extra would be useful before my dear Papa croaks his last."

"Well, Sophia Darling isn't showing many signs of—er…croaking."

"No, but I'm sure a reasonable advance on the occasion of her niece's marriage might be useful. A prudent husband might make it a condition of the marriage."

"My dear Cyril, the Blackwell girls might be a trifle gauche and already into their twenties, but they are hardly at their last prayers. I doubt either Blackwell or Lady Darling is that desperate about them. Especially if Calton is giving the impression of sniffing about them."

"The point is to *make* them desperate. And put Calton in his place at the same time."

A smile had begun to hover on her luscious lips. "You mean to ruin the girl and force a marriage to you."

"Only if you approve," he said, smiling. He rose and walked toward her. "It needn't change anything between us." He bent and drew her slowly to her feet. "In fact, it might provide us both with an extra little…fillip."

She turned her face up to his. "It might at that," she said huskily. "You may take me to bed, Cyril, and tell me more."

"I thought we could plan together." He swept his hand down her back, pulling the length of her body against him. "I may need your help in getting her alone."

"Which one?"

"Does it matter?"

"It might to Calton."

"True, and worth discovering." He stroked down her throat and inside her robe toward her breasts.

"It will be difficult in London."

"I heard some talk of a party in the country, at the Wennings' place."

"Harcourt. Of course. The Blackwells are bound to go since it will be full of Wenning's boring diplomatic friends. On the other hand, perhaps it's time I renewed my old friendship with Grace Wenning and accepted her invitation. I wasn't going to since she has become so dull. No one would believe she was once so amusing. Perhaps you could escort me."

"Will that not be your husband's duty?" he inquired, unfastening the ribbons of her robe.

"Not if I don't tell him I am going. Besides, he'll be quite at home with his pigs up in Yorkshire by now. Are you going to take me to bed, Cyril, or am I to be taken on the floor like some doxy?"

"Floor," he said, sweeping her up and laying her there.

She laughed, winding her naked limbs about him. "Now tell me all…"

He didn't, of course. Not quite all. Such as that he already knew it was the younger sister they would pursue. Nor that he would have pursued her whether or not she would inherit her aunt's money. Nor that as he made passionate love to his mistress, it was Josephine Blackwell's piquant, provoking beauty he imagined beneath him.

CHAPTER SIX

HARCOURT, THE EARL of Wenning's chief seat, proved to be a large, gracious house, most of which was built in the previous century around a medieval great hall, now the impressive entrance foyer. It was surrounded by formal gardens, a maze, and what looked like a wildflower meadow, leading to woodland.

Since they had arrived rather late the previous evening, neither Aunt Darling nor Helena rose early, leaving Josephine to join her father in the breakfast parlor where, as well as her hosts, she encountered several other old friends, including Sir Joseph and Lady Sayle. The ladies invited her to join them in the garden where they were entertaining their children, while Wenning took her father and Sir Joe off to his library.

After half an hour or so of baby worship, Josephine wandered off to explore the grounds. It was a bright, clear day and so warm in the direct sunshine that she lay down among the wildflowers—there were still poppies among the harebells and hawkbit blooms and the general prettiness pleased her.

Here, amongst the quiet beauty, she thought back over last night's last conversation with Helena in their shared bedchamber.

"If I went away," Helena had said suddenly, just as Josephine was about to fall asleep, "would you come with me?"

"Away where?" Josephine had demanded.

"Abroad. Somewhere I could have the baby secretly and have

it adopted."

Josephine had propped herself up on one elbow, peering at her sister in the darkness, wishing one candle at least was still lit. "Would you be happy having the child adopted?"

"It is the best of the bad choices I have."

"Perhaps," Josephine had allowed. "And yes, of course, I would come. Does this mean you have decided to tell Papa?"

"Of course not! I could not bear…" Helena had gathered a shaky breath. "Lord Calton has said he would help me. He has trusted people abroad who would handle everything discreetly. Then you will be safe from scandal, and Papa will not be shamed."

"And you will have lost your child."

"Don't, Josephine," Helena had said harshly. "This is hard enough, and I don't think I could do it alone. But if you were with me…"

"Of course, I would be with you. Whatever you do, I will be with you. I just feel bad lying to Papa and to Darling Aunt."

"With luck, the lying will be minimal. We will just need to accept an invitation, and once we arrive find an excuse to send home the servants and chaperones they send with us. And stay a while longer, perhaps, than was initially arranged."

"It might work," Josephine had allowed.

Going over it in her head, she still thought it might work. And it probably was Helena's best chance. Only a nagging feeling at the back of her mind worried at her. That it was wrong. That Helena, who must have loved the father of her child, however briefly, would regret the loss of her child.

And that they would be putting a lot of trust in Lord Calton.

Even at the thought of him, butterflies rose in her stomach. She had ridden out unsuitable physical attractions before. The Italian tenor. The embassy footman. Prince Metternich. There had never been any accounting for such crushes. In most cases, she had rarely said more than a word to any of them, and she knew from experience that such feelings faded from lack of nourishment. But they had never taken over her every thought as Calton did.

He was different. She *liked* him. She liked his humor, his smile, and his understated kindness. She liked him for the attention he gave to Helena, even while she wished it were focused on herself. She liked the way he looked, the way he felt, and smelled. God help her, she had loved his weight upon her, between her legs when he had kissed her.

She closed her eyes, reliving the memory so vividly that she could almost smell that distinctive male scent, clean and yet earthy. Her whole body heated and tingled. She even imagined his presence close by, perhaps admiring her, she thought wistfully.

Disconcerted by her own imaginings, she opened her eyes. And saw him gazing down at her, his fair hair falling over his handsome face, his eyes lazily amused.

She sat up, gasping. He was still there, not a dream.

"What the devil are you doing here?" she demanded.

"Admiring your choice of couch," he said and folded himself down beside her among the flowers. "I nearly trod on you."

She eyed him suspiciously. "You are staying here at Harcourt?"

"You needn't sound so astonished. Wenning and I are old friends."

"You were not at breakfast," she accused.

"I slept in," he said blandly. "Due to an excess of debauchery the night before."

She smiled. "Liar."

His eyebrows lifted. "You think me incapable of abusing my hosts' hospitality?"

"No. But you wouldn't tell me about it. So, I know you're making it up to shock me."

"Why would I do that?"

"I have no idea, but I suspect you do it a lot."

"I was only trying to compete with whatever intense

thoughts held you in such thrall."

She flushed. "Merely happy memories of times long past." Hastily, she changed the subject. "Helena told me of your offer to help us go abroad. You are being very kind."

His gaze broke from hers, regarding the flowers toward the woods. "Not kind. More of a *there but for the grace of God* moment. I hope someone would look out for anyone I did not or could not help."

"I suppose you must have been very debauched," she said thoughtfully, and immediately wished the earth would swallow her up.

He gave a crack of laughter. "I thought I just pretended."

"You pretend to be worse than you are. I'm sure you are still pretty bad."

His eyes returned to hers, reflecting the sun and the flowers. "Do you mind?"

"It is none of my business," she muttered.

"Perhaps you think it is if Helena accepts my offer of help."

"I seem to trust you. So does she, more to the point."

He regarded her, pulling idly at a harebell until the stem broke into his hand. "And yet you don't like the plan."

"I don't. But I can't think of a better one if she won't confront the father. I don't even know if he is a scoundrel, just that she must have loved him."

"I don't believe he is a scoundrel."

She gazed at him with a hint of dread. "You know who he is. Or think you do. Did she tell you?"

"Lord, no. I have my suspicions, and I would say he loves her. What I'm not sure of, is whether or not she loves him. So, I am asking you."

"Who?" she demanded. "Who do you believe it is?"

He sighed. "I swear you to secrecy."

"Of course," she said impatiently."

"Andre de Talley."

Her jaw dropped. "*Talley?* That's ridiculous!"

"Why?"

Her mouth opened, then closed again. "I don't know."

"Did you think he loved you?"

"Don't be silly," she snapped. "I thought he was a friend, not a… Talley? Are you sure?"

"Mostly."

"Then I must speak to him at once." She made to rise, but his long fingers closed around her wrist, jerking her back down so that she fell against him. For an instant, he held her back against his broad chest, his arm across the front of her body, and she was flooded with pleasure and excitement.

And then he released her, and she pulled away as though indignant. Which, in one sense, she was.

"You must not tell him anything," Calton said. "If you do, you will spoil everything."

"I fail to see how *everything* could be more spoiled than it is now."

"Consider. Why has she not told him herself? He is not married. He clearly cares for her family, and most especially for her. And yet she keeps her secret. Why would she do that?"

Josephine could see no reason at all, except pregnancy-induced insanity. "You appear to have the answers."

"What if she does not believe he wants to marry her? She has pride. She does not wish to be married only because of what she probably regards as a mistake. Or is afraid he regards as a mistake."

Josephine wanted to deny such idiocy, but after a moment, she nodded slowly. "She might think so. It might have happened when we were in Brighton, only he did not stay for long. And then we did not see him in London until Darling Aunt's ball."

"So, if you tell him now, what will he do?"

"Confront her. Ask her to marry him. *Insist* she marries him."

"Which is exactly what she does not want. She will refuse him."

Josephine scrubbed at her forehead, as though it could somehow send some sense from her brain to her sister's. "Of all the proud, stupid, pointless…"

"In her place," Calton interrupted, "what would *you* do?"

"I would never have got that close to Talley in the first place," she muttered.

"Not to Talley, perhaps."

But she had *almost* been that close to Calton. In his room at Renwick's Hotel. Sense had already fled her mind in favor of her body's blind lust. Another few minutes of such kisses and caresses, and would she not have been utterly seduced, bedded, and in as much trouble as Helena? She liked to think she would have found strength and sanity in time, but…

Ignoring his last words, she said abruptly, "Then what would you have us do?"

He twirled the harebell stem between his fingers. "Find out if she still loves him. If she does, then we can combine to throw them together, encourage him to offer for her *before* he knows about the baby."

She thought about that. "It might work. And if she has taken Talley in dislike?"

"Then we can revert to the plan for her to go abroad."

She frowned. "I will need to make an excuse for us to go back to London."

"There is no need. Talley is coming here tomorrow."

She blinked. "He is?"

He smiled faintly and reached across to thread the harebell into the hair above her ear. "The French Ambassador is a friend of mine."

"Of course, he is," she managed, afraid to breathe as his fingers moved gently against her scalp.

He leaned back and rose to his feet, then held down his hand to her. "Shall we go back to the house before Grace sends out a search party?"

She could not avoid taking his hand. She didn't even want to, though she hid her pleasure in his touch, in his strength, immediately slipping free as soon as she was on her feet.

"Grace will not notice," she assured him. "She is too busy child-worshipping." Another thought struck her. "Oh dear, I hope all this doting on the little ones does not distress Helena. Perhaps I should warn her. I don't think either of us realized how many children there would be."

He offered her his arm. "She is lucky to have you to look after her."

She took his arm—it would have been rude not to—but cast him a sardonic smile. "That isn't what you said when we first met."

"Isn't it?" he asked. "It should have been."

Something else struck her. "Wait though. Is our plan fair to Talley? Should he not know everything *before* he offers?"

"No," Calton replied. "It is his responsibility, and it should make no difference to his feelings."

"Then why did he not offer for her at once? In Brighton?"

Calton shrugged. "I gather he is expecting promotion from this posting in London. Perhaps he needs it to support a wife. We can ask him. Once everything is settled."

CALTON REGARDED HIS visit to Harcourt as his farewell to England for at least a year. Once he had sorted out the Blackwell-Talley problem, he could proceed to Europe with a clear conscience, waved off by his friends.

But life had a way of growing unnecessarily complicated.

He had just sat down to luncheon, noticing that Josephine Blackwell had removed the flower from her hair and being disproportionately sorry for it, when a carriage had pulled up on the terrace outside the dining room window. And from it stepped Cyril Gough, a man both nosy and unsavory, according to Calton's discreet inquiries. And Gough turned to hand down a lady he had no desire to meet again—Selina Reddington.

Calton was a man of the world. It was hardly the first time he had met a former mistress in a social gathering. But Selina's attitude made him uneasy. He even doubted her presence would rein in the worst impulses of her escort, who was generally not the first choice of a hostess.

Calton's own reputation was hardly the purest, but he never *molested* anyone.

Beside him, Grace Wenning rose at once to welcome the new guests, causing Calton to stand as well.

"Gough?" he murmured.

"Well, I invited the husband," Grace replied, "and appear to have the understudy." She bustled off, and Calton sat down again.

Andre de Talley did not appear until almost teatime, having ridden from London on the horse Calton had lent him, with his modest luggage, presumably, in his saddle bags. Annoyingly, since pall mall was over, Calton could only watch from his bedchamber window, unable to see the reaction of Helena Blackwell.

Tea was served in a pleasant salon that caught the late afternoon sun through its large French windows leading onto the terrace.

"Why, Calton, what a pleasure," Selina Reddington drawled as soon as he walked in. "Still not made it to France?"

"Are you pushing me out of the country, ma'am?" Calton inquired, bowing over her hand.

"Hardly, my lord! Come, sit by me and tell me how you know the Wennings. I expect you were also at the feet of the incomparable Grace?"

"I still am," Calton said. He would have moved to collect a cup of tea from his hostess, using that as an excuse to ignore Selina's invitation. However, Lady Wenning's helpful new sister-in-law, Lady Darblay, ferried it to him with a smile, leaving him with no civil option but to smile and sit beside Selina.

Gough, he saw with irritation, had already positioned himself between the Blackwell sisters. At least Talley, who had clearly changed with haste from his riding attire and washed the dust of the road from his person, sat on Helena's other side. Calton could not resist glancing at Josephine, who was smiling faintly and deliberately, he suspected, not looking at him while she listened to Gough.

"A penny for them," Selina said lightly.

"My thoughts? Worthless, I assure you." He returned his considering gaze to her. "I'm surprised to see you here, too. I would not have thought this your kind of party."

"Too serious for me?" Selina suggested, apparently amused. "Grace was not always so serious, if you recall. We were close once." She lowered her voice. "Though between you and me, she has grown virtuous and dull."

"Always virtuous and never dull," he said gently.

"Or you would have found a way through her armor?" Selina drawled.

"I wouldn't let the vulgarity of your escort rub off on you," he murmured. "Particularly not on the subject of your hostess. Might I pass you a scone?"

As tea progressed, he was glad to see both Blackwell sisters accompany Talley outside to the formal gardens. It began a general exodus in that direction, so Calton strolled out to observe—a new role to him.

Mr. Blackwell seemed unconcerned about his daughters being in Talley's company, even when Josephine allowed herself to fall behind and move back toward the house leaving her sister alone with him.

Nicely done. He sauntered in her direction to tell her so, although Grace's brother Darblay got to her a few seconds earlier. Marriage had clearly not blinded Darblay to the charms of other women, Calton thought irritably. Although on the whole, he would rather Darblay than Gough sniffing around her.

Darblay, however, did not seem to be sniffing so much as making her laugh, and Calton rather liked to see Josephine laugh.

And when Darblay enthusiastically beckoned his wife to join them, Calton relaxed his vigilance and remembered that he liked all the Darblays.

"Hope," he said suddenly, referring to the youngest sibling. "Did I not hear that Hope was married?"

"In the summer," Lady Darblay said. "To Oatland."

"The reclusive duke," Calton observed. "I suppose that is why they are not here."

Darblay grinned. "He's not that reclusive, just pleasantly eccentric. They're off on an extended wedding journey, so you may run into them in Europe."

"When do you go, my lord?" Josephine asked. He probably imagined the anxiety in her voice, although she *would* be anxious for him to deliver the help he had promised Helena, should events here not work out as they hoped.

"After the party," he said vaguely, though for some reason, he did not feel quite so determined about it. "When my affairs are suitably settled. Excuse me."

INEVITABLY, AFTER DINNER, the unmarried young ladies were begged to entertain. Calton had always found this a particularly trying part of country house parties—and some Town parties, too—for there seemed to be little requirement for those displaying their accomplishments to actually possess any. He cringed for some, tried to cover his ears for most, and generally found a reason to slip away until the whole horrible cacophony had stopped.

Accordingly, he found a seat closest to the drawing room door and smiled blandly at his host when Wenning raised one sardonic eyebrow.

Rollo Darblay threw himself into the chair beside Calton, lowering himself as though trying to hide. "Fancy a game of cards?"

"I'd love one," Calton murmured without moving, "but her ladyship would spit us both alive."

Fortunately, the first young lady only played on the pianoforte. She played a lullaby like a march, presumably to get it over with more quickly, but at least she played the correct notes, and Calton felt his lips twitch.

"I've got a theory," Darblay murmured, leaning closer during the polite applause, "that some young ladies are married solely to prevent them caterwauling in public or destroying perfectly serviceable musical instruments. It's a kindness to society. Oh, confound it, this one's going to sing."

Surreptitiously, Darblay passed him two small, wrinkled pieces of linen. Calton's breath caught on laughter when he saw Darblay casually stuff similar pieces into his own ears.

From his somewhat detached position at the back of the room, Calton watched proud and frequently tone-deaf mamas push their offspring forward to entertain. It took a while to realize that no one was pushing either of the Blackwell sisters who, presumably, knew their limitations.

It was only as the mother of the first girl began to offer the services of her daughter for a second time that Lady Darling said with a hint of desperation, "As I recall, you used to play very well, Helena. Would you not give us a last song?"

"Oh yes, we would love you to," Grace said at once, with well-hidden relief. "Please, Miss Blackwell."

Helena hesitated, as other voices joined in the polite pleas. She gave in gracefully, rising and smiling, though she said, "Only if Josephine will sing to cover my mistakes!"

"A duet," Grace exclaimed. "Perfect."

Josephine looked positively alarmed. Calton found himself holding his breath, wishing for some reason that she would refuse. As though he did not want her diminished, reduced to the status of the other indifferent performers.

Andre de Talley murmured something in her ear. Helena

pulled her to her feet and dragged her toward the piano. Calton could see the older sister talking quietly and rapidly to the younger whose rigid shoulders finally relaxed, although her head bowed in apparent defeat.

Calton wanted to shout at them all, including Helena, to let her be. He wanted to haul her off to the gardens instead and watch her laugh by moonlight rather than cringe. For the first time, he was tempted to use Darblay's earplugs, had even lifted one hand casually to his ear, when Helena began to play the pianoforte with rather more skill than most.

And then Josephine began to sing.

It was a gentle, plaintive ballad, sung in Italian, but that wasn't what froze his hand at his ear and the breath in his body. It was Josephine's voice, pure and clear and sweet enough to melt every bone in the room.

He lowered his hand, forcing himself to breathe, and slowly shifted his gaze to the singer. She looked straight toward the back of the room, probably at some point above his and Darblay's heads. And he knew instinctively that she could only perform if she did not see her audience.

And she was more than good. Together, the sisters turned a sad little love song into a haunting, captivating air. Helena played with more than skill. She played with feeling. And Josephine… Emotions chased each other across her face, expressing the words of the song as eloquently as that delicious voice. Shivers ran down his spine. The hair on his neck, on his arms, prickled, and he could not look away.

Almost imperceptibly, her gaze moved, lowering slowly to Calton's face. And his heart shattered.

CHAPTER SEVEN

Alone in Wenning's library, with only the light of the fire and one lamp to guide him, Calton reached for the brandy once more and splashed a generous amount into his glass. He was aware he was drinking too much, but it didn't seem to make much difference to his already befuddled brain. It certainly didn't dull the bizarre mixture of pain and euphoria that had engulfed him when Josephine had sung. When she had sung to him.

Of course, she had not *really* sung to him. She had just sung, and his face had got in the way of the wall that was her first choice. But the knowledge didn't change his feelings. He shied away from those.

The Blackwells had won delighted applause for their performance, and had even obliged with another, an amusing traditional air with a foot-tapping rhythm that had made everyone clap along and laugh. Calton suspected he had kept the same smile fixed on his face throughout. Only long service in the art of hiding his feelings had enabled him to get through the next couple of hours.

He had even given Josephine her night candle when she and Helena had retired for the evening. And then shared a late card game and a glass of brandy with several of the younger men, who had, by now, left him alone to brood with the rest of the brandy.

Music had done that to him before—dragged out to the surface the emotion he had safely buried. Grief for Francis, for his mother, fury at his father, some callow lost love he had long since forgotten. But this…it was as though Josephine had been central to the surge of emotion. It had caught everything from his past, grief, regret, joy. But mostly joy, mostly…love.

For her.

It wasn't real, of course. It was merely a moment, inspired by her unexpectedly beautiful voice and the power of the music, and would be gone when next they met.

Really, it would.

And if it is not? What then? I go to Europe and leave her here for some snake like Gough to gobble up?

And if Gough is a snake, what am I? A rake and a bit of a scoundrel who could not be faithful to a wife if I tried. She deserves better.

So long as she gets better, and not Gough or some other…

It is not my decision. It is hers and her father's. Nothing has happened that need make me change my plans.

And yet, he had the feeling everything had already changed, and that both appalled and excited him.

He raised the brandy to his lips and glanced up. A ghostly figure flitted past him with a book in its hand and curled up in the chair on the other side of the fire. A ghost with Josephine Blackwell's face.

He must have stirred, for she suddenly looked right at him and her mouth fell open.

"You!"

"I was about to say the same thing." It might not have been witty repartee but at least his words didn't slur.

She wore only a nightgown and a thin dressing robe, her gorgeous hair tumbling free about her shoulders. "I thought the library was empty!"

"Sadly not. What is it? Could you not sleep?"

She shook her head. "No, and I couldn't read without disturbing Helena, so I came in search of somewhere warm."

He picked up the decanter and waved it at her. "Brandy?"

She shook her head, her smile both amused and uncertain. He wanted to wind her luxurious hair around his hand, his neck, to bury his nose and mouth there. It would feel like silk and smell like…her. Like Josephine.

"You sing beautifully. I never expected that."

"That I might have an accomplishment?" she asked, lightly teasing.

"Not an accomplishment, a talent, a beauty. Another beauty."

She flushed in the firelight, or at least she seemed to. "Are you drunk, my lord?"

"I should be," he admitted, regarding his glass with disfavor. "But the god of brandy rejects my prayers."

A frown flickered across her brow. "You were sad. While I was singing."

"You touched my heart," he said honestly. At least it was a welcome sign of drunkenness, although he was sober enough to wish the words unsaid.

"It is a moving song," she allowed.

"Sung from your heart. You have hidden depths, Josephine Blackwell. Who was he?"

She blinked. "Who was who?"

"The man you loved."

"No one. Unless you count a very passing admiration for a footman and Prince Metternich. You mistake imagination for reality."

He didn't think so, but he let it go. It was not his business, and he had no right to jealousy. He finished his brandy instead, knowing he should get up and leave.

She said, "I think you might be right about Talley and Helena. She was definitely pleased to see him at tea, although she said little to him. I haven't had much chance to speak to her privately about it, though."

He nodded, dredging up something else he had needed to say to her. "Gough. Don't trust him. Or Selina Reddington. People like them spread gossip like poison."

"Darling Aunt—that is my Aunt Darling—told Papa Mrs. Reddington was your mistress." She unwound herself from the chair. "I should not have said that. I'm sorry."

"Then why did you? Do think I'll forget your indiscretion by morning? I won't you know. Though for what it's worth, Selina Reddington is not my mistress."

"Oh."

Did he imagine the relief in her voice? "She was once, but we parted, and that is all I will say."

"Then why say that much?" she demanded—with some cause since it was hardly appropriate conversation for an unmarried young lady.

"Because we are friends. Because I am no saint. And because…" He broke off with a laugh. "Well, maybe that's enough becauses."

Now that she was sitting up straight and no longer clutched the robe closed, he could see the shape of her breasts through her nightgown. Full yet pert and unbearably alluring. Forcing himself, he brought his gaze back to her face and found her eyes wide and almost…frightened.

It was the last that gave him the impetus. He rose without a stagger. "I should leave you to your book. Good night, Miss—"

"Oh, no, you were here first." She jumped up, grasping the robe closed once more, and the book fell to the ground.

They both bent to pick it up, but he was faster. A flattened harebell had fluttered out of it. He rose with both of them and held them out to her.

"It would not have lasted in water," she muttered, all but snatching them. "They wilt so quickly."

"They do," he agreed, while a stupid, vain possibility hammered in his mind. Could the man who had inspired the emotion of her song, the man he was still sure had also inspired her love, be *him*?

Testing his theory, he took her free hand and bowed over it. He let his fingers trail up her palm to her wrist. Her pulse galloped. He could not stop himself from pressing his lips there, too. Her skin was so soft, scented like summer flowers and sheer Josephine.

He straightened, taking in her quick, panting breath that made her breasts rise and fall so desirably. Lust surged through him with such intensity that he knew he had to go, urgently, while he could still walk.

He would have managed it, too, had she not taken an involuntary step toward him. "Please," she said brokenly.

"Please?" He closed his eyes against temptation, but he seemed to have lowered his head, for his face brushed against her hair and he smiled because it really did feel like silk. It smelled adorable, too, like her skin, which was warm and delicate against his lips and tasted of heat and desire. "One of us has to leave this room," he whispered. "Quickly. Or I will kiss you. And you may need that damned pistol to make me stop."

A gasp that was half-laughter shook her. "I couldn't find another bullet for it."

"What a pity," he groaned, inhaling her breath as she moved her lips so close to his. "What a desperate, terrible pity…" And then his mouth brushed hers and sank deeply, sweetly into bliss.

EVEN BEFORE HIS mouth touched hers, Josephine had been incapable of walking to the door. Her insides seemed to have melted and her limbs felt like liquid lead. A sweet, heaviness sat in the pit of her stomach, radiating heat and need and pleasure. And then he kissed her.

Something like a sob escaped her lips as they opened and welcomed his. There was none of the sensual calculation of his first kiss at the hotel. This was sheer, animal instinct, hungry, raw, and utterly irresistible. Without meaning to, she pushed herself against the hard length of his body, and his powerful arms held her there, his hands running possessively up and down her back as he devoured her mouth like a starving man.

She clutched his face between her hands, drove her fingers through his hair, and kissed him back. She knew she was all emotion and no skill, but it didn't seem to bother him, for a lustful growl vibrated from his throat into her own body. His tongue wound with hers, playing, teasing, taking, even while his hands roamed further over her hips and waist and the sides of her breasts.

She barely noticed him tug aside the robe, but she moaned as he found her breast through the thin lawn of her night rail, sweetly caressing her nipple. His open mouth left hers, dragging across her jaw to her throat, trailing kisses downward to meet his hand.

His other hand was on her rear, pulling her against his hips, which moved languidly, stroking his obvious arousal against her abdomen. His leg shifted between hers, and she gasped just as his mouth returned to hers. Her whole being seemed to be in flames, some wild, intensely physical pleasure rising, clamoring within her.

He swept her feet right off the floor. She was barely conscious of her dressing gown landing in a heap, for he strode to the sofa and sat with her in his lap. With delight as well as desperate need, she held his head to her breast while he teased it with lips and tongue and the gentle graze of his teeth. Her fingers fisted convulsively in his hair while he dragged up her nightgown, caressing the length of her leg as he did so.

He raised his head, shifting to kiss her mouth once more. The glow of the solitary lamp reflected in his hot, clouded eyes, cast his jaw into deep shadow beneath the prominent blades of his cheekbones. His breath was at least as uneven as hers, but his passionate, sinful lips were smiling with an almost predatory triumph that excited her madly. And yet behind the desire, his eyes held a care and a gentleness that melted what was left of her sanity.

His hand stilled on her naked thigh.

"You trust me," he whispered.

"I do."

His fingers slid up her body to touch her lips. "And I am a hairsbreadth away from abusing that trust." His head lowered, not to kiss her lips but to lean his forehead against hers while his panting breath slowly calmed.

She tugged at his hair in barely understood need. "What is it? You have not hurt me."

A breath of laughter touched her lips. He raised his head. "Not yet. Not quite yet. My sweet, the door is unlocked, you are one insomniac away from ruin, and this is not the way it should be between us. I won't take away your choices."

She wanted to seduce him. She wanted to hit him or stalk regally away. But he gathered her close against his chest and smoothed down her nightgown.

"Is this about Helena?" she asked shakily.

He shook his head. "It is about you and me." His hand cupped her cheek with a tenderness that made her want to weep. "This moment is not over between us—unless you declare it so. We are…pausing. For reflection."

Reflection was the last thing she needed. It was the last thing she wanted him to be doing either.

All she grasped was that she had gone willingly into his arms, happy—nay, desperate—to be seduced by him, and he was rejecting her. Because she had done something wrong, or because she was not attractive enough.

His lips brushed hers. "Don't let it be over."

At last, pride came to her rescue. She clambered out of his lap, fighting the sense of loss. "I believe you have already declared it so."

She moved toward her fallen robe, but though she hadn't been aware of him moving behind her, it was he who whisked it off the floor and held it for her. She slid her arms into it, wishing him far away, wishing his nearness did not melt her, wishing he would take her back into his arms and tell her…What? Anything. Just make love to her.

Only, she couldn't allow it now. She wouldn't. And he clearly didn't want her.

What did I do?

I don't know what to do…

He drew the robe around her and stood for a moment looking down at her. But she could not bear his scrutiny. She whisked herself out of his hold, sweeping up the book she had come here to read.

"Good night, my lord," she said distantly and probably ridiculously as she swept toward the door with all the dignity she did not feel. But of course, he was there to open that, too. He even looked outside, to make sure all was quiet before he held it wide for her, and then handed her a lit stub of a candle that might just make it to her bedchamber before dying.

It was the most difficult journey she had ever made. And when, eventually, she cast herself face down on her bed in the darkness, she knew there was no way she would ever sleep.

SNEAKING BACK TO his own bedchamber just before dawn, Gough knew he thrived on the intrigue. He had never quite managed the feat of having two mistresses on the go, as it were, at once, but he rather thought he would enjoy the juggling act. If Selina found out about Josephine Blackwell, she would drop him, of course. Not that there was anything to find out yet. But when there was, he thought he might tell Josephine about Selina, just so that she would know she was not the only one, that her survival hung by a very thin thread.

He liked that idea. God, how she would cling to him.

A sound from the staircase caused him to dart into his bedchamber. From sheer curiosity, he left his door open a crack to see who was wandering about at this hour. Surely it was too early for the servants to be about?

A solitary man wandered past his door in the darkness. It was impossible to make out his features, but just by the way the dark figure moved, sure and easy and unconsciously arrogant, he knew it was the Earl of Calton.

Interesting. What was he doing wandering about the house at this hour? If he had not come up the stairs, he would have assumed his nocturnal activities were similar to Gough's own, but the bedchambers were all on this floor.

Perhaps he was reduced to bothering the maids. Gough grinned. He rather liked that idea, for he had just enjoyed Calton's former mistress.

CHAPTER EIGHT

A LTHOUGH SHE HADN'T expected to sleep at all, she must have done, for she definitely woke up to sunshine in the room and the sounds of Helena moving about.

Josephine kept her eyes closed, just to be able to think in peace for a few minutes. The events of last night never seemed to have left her, so it was not a question of recalling them, but at least sleep seemed to have imbued them with greater understanding.

Calton had not been rejecting her so much as looking after her. And if she had been seduced to within an inch of her honor, so had he. He merely had the experience to know where their behavior had been going and to stop it.

Dear God, what must he think of me? Of my family? Helena is already with child, and I threw myself at him as though determined to get into the same condition.

Embarrassment washed over her in waves. Which at least prevented her dwelling on the exquisite pleasure of Calton's kisses and bold caresses…mostly.

"Are you awake, Jo?" Helena asked. "If I don't eat soon, I shall be sick. Don't ask me how that works, because I don't know."

Josephine threw off the bedcovers and hauled herself upright. She washed and dressed hastily, with Helena's help. They fastened each other's hooks, pronounced each other respectable, and sallied forth together to the breakfast parlor, without troubling either Aunt Darling or their father.

Josephine's heart beat uncomfortably fast as they approached the parlor, for she had no idea how she would face Lord Calton.

Friendly dignity, she told herself. Though how that was to be achieved, she had no idea. Too soon, Helena was all but dragging her into the room.

But she need not have worried. Their host was present, tucking into a plate of eggs and bacon and sausages. So was Sir Joe Sayle, Talley, and one of the debutantes whose name Josephine had forgotten, along with her mother. But no sign of Calton.

So, it was easy to wish the company good morning and follow Helena to the sideboard. Starving as Helena claimed to be, she took only a poached egg and a slice of toast. But at least she was eating something. For a couple of weeks before, she had seemed to be starving herself.

Having a larger appetite, Josephine spent longer at the sideboard. So, she had her back to the door when Calton's deep voice said cheerfully, "Good morning, all."

Immediately, her heart started hammering again. She did not know whether to bolt for the table or stay where she was until he got there. And then he *was* there, damnably large and gorgeous.

"Miss Blackwell. May I help you to some beef?"

"Thank you, no," she managed, keeping her voice light. "I will just have a cup of coffee."

Before she could move around him to do so, he poured her a cup and passed it to her. Their fingers touched, and as her eyes flew to his face, something small and cold passed from his hand to hers.

"Thank you," she managed, hiding the tiny object in her palm while she carried her cup and saucer in one hand and her plate in the other.

She sat down beside Helena, and as soon she could discreetly do so, she glanced down at her left hand in her lap and opened it to reveal a small, metal ball. The bullet he had once emptied from her pistol.

Her breath caught on surprised laughter. He sat opposite her and smiled amiably. But his eyes danced as they met hers, inviting her to share the joke. And suddenly, wonderingly, her shame vanished into peculiar happiness.

"This moment is not over."

JOSEPHINE FINALLY FOUND her moment to assess her sister's feelings as they walked together in the formal gardens later that morning. Though they had escaped the noise and mayhem of the children playing around the terraces with their doting parents, their laughter could still be heard in the distance.

"Do they bother you?" Josephine asked. "Other people's happy children?"

For the first time that she had seen, Helena's arm crossed protectively over her stomach. "No. I like it. Though I suppose it is a bittersweet liking since it is something I will never know."

Josephine's throat tightened. "Never is a very long time, Lena."

Helena nodded but said nothing.

Josephine was wondering how best to bring up the subject of Andre de Talley, when her sister saved her the trouble.

"What were you and Talley talking about in the hall when I came upon you?" Helena asked, rather carefully casual.

Josephine shrugged. "Oh, I was just teasing him about his growing influence with the ambassador, since he managed to obtain leave of absence."

Helena smiled faintly. "I believe he fears it means he is easily replaceable."

"Not our Talley." She looked directly at her sister. "But…don't you think he is different somehow since he arrived in England."

Helena cast her a quick glance, then bent to sniff a late rose.

"Different, how?"

"Oh, I don't know. Like a grown-up, I suppose! When we used to like him because he wasn't stuffy like the other diplomats."

Helena gave a faint smile. "We were really only children ourselves in Vienna."

"Well, he is definitely a man now."

"Why do you say that?" Helena asked quickly.

Josephine shrugged. "Because he is different with us. With you." Although her words were for effect, they were also true. Once she truly watched, she had easily seen what Calton had already noticed. Tally was subtly different with Helena, just a little more solicitous, more protective, his smile a little more tender than the merely friendly one he bestowed upon Josephine.

"Is he?" Helena's careless words somehow bore a hint of wistfulness.

Josephine took her turn sniffing the rose, though it carried little scent. "At the risk of spoiling a delightful friendship, I believe he might have a *tendre* for you."

"Talley?" Helena said breathlessly. "I see no reason why you would imagine such a thing. His *tendre* might as easily be for you."

"No, it isn't," Josephine stated. "Of course, he is still my old friend, but it is you he watches, you who lights up his eyes. Do you like him?"

Helena's fair skin was pink. "Of course, I like him."

Josephine nudged her. "In *that* way?"

Without warning, Helena grasped her elbow in a hard grip. "Don't you dare say anything to him, Jo. Not a single thing. You must not interfere."

"Oh, I won't," Josephine assured her. "I learned my lesson with Calton. Although," she couldn't help adding, "that hasn't worked out so badly, has it?"

Helena laughed shakily. "You are incorrigible."

"And you are silly. Talley feels his lowly position compared to yours. Why don't you just put the poor man out of his misery and tell him how you feel?"

Helena gestured to her own body. "Like this?" she said in despair.

Josephine bit her tongue, being damned sure Talley was the cause of *this*. Instead, she said, "Lena. If you love him, trust him."

As she, somehow, trusted Lord Calton.

⋙✖⋘

IN THE AFTERNOON, some of the younger people rode out with Lord Wenning to see an abbey ruin on the edge of a scenic lake that bounded his property to the south. Calton, who had pleasant memories of swimming in the lake as a schoolboy, was more than happy to accompany the expedition, especially since both Blackwell sisters and Talley were part of it.

Oddly enough, the strength of his feelings for Josephine no longer terrified him. It was as if their encounter in the library had banished all the silly paraphernalia with which he had surrounded his life and left only the stark truth. That he wanted her more than anyone or anything ever. In fact, holding her in his arms, passionate and willing, he still wasn't sure how he had made himself stop.

Or why. For in truth, it seemed the stopping rather than the beginning that had offended her.

When she had left, he had gone outside to cool his ardor in a brisk walk that had turned into a run and ended with him lying flat on his back under the stars, smiling because she could be part of his life. The most important part. She could be with him, his to cherish and protect and love. To laugh with and adventure with...

He could have taken her in the library, and perhaps he should, for assuredly, he meant to marry her. Though perhaps he had flung enough at her for one day.

She rode ahead of him with her sister and Talley, which meant he could admire her seat on the horse, the slope of her shoulders, the slender column of her neck, which he ached to kiss.

"You used to always lead the way, Calton," Selina Reddington murmured beside him. "Can it be you have turned into a slow top since our time together?"

"Perhaps I was always a slow top," he said lightly. "And I have no reason to believe Wenning will lead us the wrong way on his own land. How are you, Selina?"

He turned his head with reluctance to look at her and read the conflict in her face quite easily. On one hand, she wanted to assure him of her continued boredom, which was probably the truth. On the other, she wanted him to understand how happy she was with her new lover.

In the end, she waved one careless hand. "As you see. And you, my lord?"

"Likewise."

She sighed. "I do hope we are not about to discuss the weather next."

"It is why we parted, Selina," he said gently. "We no longer have anything to say to one another."

"Talking was never on our agenda," she said sardonically.

"That is another reason." There had always been a hint of desperation in Selina's passion. He had recognized her unhappiness but never his own until now. "You are bored, Selina. If you can do no more, make the best of a life with your husband. Or leave him honestly."

With that, he spurred ahead to join Wenning.

His opportunity to speak to Josephine came while they strolled around the ruins and came face to face at what had once been a huge, arched window. Immediately, she blushed adorably, and he wished everyone else at Jericho so that he might finish what they had begun last night.

It was clear she didn't know quite how to face him, and yet

she stood her ground with a courage he could only admire.

"My friend Dornan painted this once," he said. "At sunrise. I wonder if Wenning still has it?"

"The light is beautiful with the reflections in the lake behind." She took a step nearer, and his senses rejoiced. But she only said, "Helena has gone down to the lake."

"With…?"

"Yes," Josephine said. "She does care for him, and I'm sure you are right. With luck, there will be no need to go abroad."

"I'm told it is more comfortable to have the lying-in in familiar surroundings with family and friends close by."

"I would rather it that way."

He offered her his arm. "Shall we walk down to the lake? Very slowly."

A smile flickered across the lips that had kissed him so deliciously only a few hours ago. "Very," she agreed.

Five minutes later, they were rewarded by the sight of Helena and Talley standing very close together, talking earnestly. He held her hand clasped in his and pressed it to his lips. She lifted her face, and Calton tugged Josephine away.

She grinned up at him. "How clever are we?"

"Very," he said gravely. "So long as nothing else goes wrong." Annoyingly, for he would have liked to take her in his arms at that point, he could hear voices and rustling footsteps approaching. He raised his voice a little louder as a warning to the couple at the water's edge. "I believe the others are coming with us."

CYRIL GOUGH, WHO had been about to pursue Josephine around to the outside of the arched window at a discreet distance, couldn't quite believe his ears. As he strolled along the inner side of the window, he was irritated to hear her voice already speaking softly to someone. Stepping closer to the stone, he made out her words.

"…am sure you are right. With luck, there will be no need to go abroad."

And a deep, male voice answered in equally low, intimate tones. "I'm told it is more comfortable to have the lying-in in familiar surroundings with family and friends close by."

"I would rather it that way," Josephine said.

"Shall we walk down to the lake? Very slowly."

Calton. It's bloody Calton. To be sure, he walked to the end of the window wall and stepped around. Arm in arm, Josephine Blackwell and the Earl of Calton were walking down toward the lake.

Damnation, he beat me there, too, Gough thought furiously. *So, it was an assignation with her I saw him returning from last night! And he's got the stupid girl with child.* Jealousy surged like a tide, for he had so wanted to be first to sample Josephine Blackwell's charms. Now, he could not even marry her, not without taking on another man's child as his heir.

Although, now he thought of it, he could overlook this if, preferably, the brat was a girl. Because her condition certainly gave a clever man several new opportunities…

He could barely wait to discuss these new developments with Selina, but unfortunately, there was no opportunity to do so until they had returned to Harcourt and he could shut himself into her bedchamber.

"Calton has got the Blackwell girl pregnant."

Selina paused, her bonnet suspended from one hand. "He's *what?*" She turned slowly to face him, looking oddly haggard in the beam of sunshine from the window. "Why ever would you think that?"

"Because I heard them." Quickly, he related what he had overheard at the abbey ruin, but her reaction was hardly what he expected.

She threw down the bonnet and sat in the armchair. "No. She

may well be pregnant, but Calton is not the father."

"My dear," he drawled, not quite pleased, "that sounds like wishful thinking."

She shrugged impatiently. "Because you don't know Calton. He goes to great efforts *not* to breed. And he has no interest in bedding innocent young girls. His tastes are far more sophisticated and besides, his peculiar sense of honor precludes it. Whoever is the father of Josephine Blackwell's child, it is not Calton."

"Then why is he involved in such discussion?"

Her lips twisted. "Quixotic chivalry, I imagine. He is more subject to it than he would like the world to think. But this is useful information, Cyril. We just have to decide how best to use it… For example, in extracting a better marriage settlement from her father."

She was right, of course. When one held such a powerful card, one didn't want to rush into playing it too soon. But at least he found an early opportunity to test the water, as it were, when he was lucky enough to run—almost literally—into Josephine on the stairs on his way down to dinner.

She catapulted onto the landing from the other guest corridor and skidded to a halt at the sight of him, trying to gather back her dignity no doubt.

A quick glance up and down the staircase assured him they were temporarily alone.

"Miss Josephine, how fortunate for me. Won't you take my arm?"

"Only if you, too, are in a hurry, sir," she said. "I seem to have dawdled and missed the rest of my family." When he proffered his arm, she only hesitated a moment before laying her fingers on his sleeve.

He smiled and patted her hand before squeezing it and drawing it more intimately into the crook of his elbow. "I must say, I am very glad to have come upon you alone. It is so difficult at these affairs to find any opportunity for private speech."

Her eyes widened. "You wish to say something privately?"

She sounded more dubious than intrigued.

He smiled. "But of course! A gentleman always has something to say to a pretty young lady. Let me begin by begging you to save me a dance at tomorrow night's ball."

"One of us will forget," she said unexpectedly. "We are much better waiting until we run into each other at the right time."

He laughed to make her believe she was witty. "How delightful you are. I will still ask for the supper dance, though I am happy to discuss the matter further."

She had a delectable neck, and now that he was close enough, he couldn't resist leaning closer with the urge to press his lips to her skin. Subtly, she eased away, increasing the distance between them once more. She even tried to increase their pace down the staircase, but he was stronger and prevented it easily.

"In fact," he murmured. "We could have that discussion this evening if you would care to meet in the garden later."

Her gaze flew to his face, and he thought, triumphantly, that he had her.

Then she said coldly, "That would hardly be proper, sir."

"Oh, come," he said, smiling, "I like a lady with a little spirit. And how else are we to get to know each other?"

Her gaze was steady. "I believe we are not," she said, making an effort to withdraw her hand, which he would not allow.

"My dear girl, I know all about you. There is no need to play off virginal airs on me."

Something sharp and heavy landed on his instep, causing him to grunt with pain.

"You are offensive," she uttered and stalked away toward the drawing room, where a footman opened the door for her and closed it again before Gough could limp after her.

By God, she did have spirit, and he would thoroughly enjoy taming her.

CHAPTER NINE

M R. GOUGH'S BEHAVIOR upset Josephine. Not just because he clearly felt entitled to accost and insult her—she had chased off such men before—but because of the nature of his insult. *Virginal airs.* Had he somehow got wind of Helena's condition and jumped to the conclusion that they were both easy pickings?

The footman at the drawing room door could not have heard the words—except her last—but he clearly spotted offensive behavior for he opened the door and closed it smartly behind her, giving her more time to find a safe refuge before admitting the noxious Gough. Without plan or thought, she scanned the room and found her sanctuary with relief.

Only later did she recall that he was standing with a group of men and that she had walked straight past Aunt Darling to get to him. Her need for *him* was instinctive. As though sensing her agitation, he glanced toward her and immediately peeled away from his companions to meet her.

She laid her trembling hand on his arm with the exact opposite of the feeling with which she had earlier taken Gough's. And Calton strolled with her to the window seat. When she had sunk onto it, he sat on the edge, turning his body toward her in a way that protected her from the sight of most in the room.

"I met Gough on the staircase," she blurted. "I think he

knows."

"Why should you think that?" he asked, his voice light and somehow steadying.

"He accused me of *playing off virginal airs.*"

"Did he, by God?" Calton's gaze was fixed on hers, carefully expressionless. "And why would you have felt the need to do so?"

"Because he invited me to dance at the ball and then to an assignation, both of which I refused."

"He won't trouble you again," Calton said calmly. "As for those *virginal airs*, it is just a saying, you know. It needn't mean anything. All the same, I'll take steps to ensure no one takes his malice seriously."

Josephine regarded him with fascination. "What steps?"

"Oh, a word here and there," he said vaguely. "But the sooner your sister's position is fixed, the easier we may all be."

He stood as a footman appeared with a tray of sherry glasses and took two with a nod of thanks. She liked that about him. He acknowledged even the smallest services, without fuss. Sitting once more, he presented her with a glass.

"Fortunately," he said, "Lady Wenning has declared informal dining this evening since we shall all retire early in preparation for tomorrow's ball. So, I may ask for the honor of taking you into dinner."

A flush rose to her face. "Thank you, but you don't need to. I am perfectly fine, now."

"I never feel obliged to do anything," he said lazily. "I am, as you know, devoted to my own pleasures."

"I know no such thing," she retorted.

"Is that an ungracious acceptance?"

She laughed. "No. But this is *gracious* acceptance. Thank you. Oh, but what if Gough pesters Helena?"

"I think we may rely on Talley. Besides, your father is in the room now. Gough will behave."

By the time they went into dinner, the incident with Gough had receded to trivial in Josephine's mind, and she merely let herself enjoy Lord Calton's company. Calton's attention. For although neither of them was rude enough to ignore the person on their other side, it was to Josephine that the earl largely devoted himself, which was a heady experience, intoxicating, even. If he flirted—and it was clearly part of his nature to do so— it was with a light touch and well within the bounds of propriety. Mostly, they talked and said nothing that anyone could not hear. And yet, when she rose from the table with the other ladies to follow her hostess to the drawing room, she was conscious chiefly of a pleasant little buzz of happiness within her.

Helena took her arm as they walked. "Lord Calton seems to be paying you particular attention."

"He is polite."

"So is Talley."

Talley had taken Helena into dinner and the pair had sat opposite Josephine and Calton.

"No more than polite?" Josephine asked.

Helena smiled, and Josephine was delighted to see that sparkle back in her eyes. "Well, perhaps a little bit more. I have been…friendlier, and he seems pleased."

Josephine squeezed her arm.

But it seemed her sister was not the only one to have noticed Calton's attentions. Aunt Darling flitted across the floor to sit beside her.

"Calton would be a great thing," she said without preamble, "but don't let yourself get carried away. He is a shocking flirt and is likely to be gone by the end of the week. Still, he likes you, anyone can see that."

"And he is not looking to marry," Josephine said, trying not to blush. "I remember."

All the same, it was a timely reminder, and one reinforced by Mrs. Reddington only a quarter of an hour later. As Josephine crossed the room toward her sister and Lady Sayle, Mrs. Reddington spoke her name, smiling, and patted the vacant seat beside her on the sofa. Since there was no polite way to refuse,

Josephine sat.

"I never had the chance to compliment you on your singing last night," Mrs. Reddington said pleasantly.

If one was being literal, she still had not done so, but Josephine merely murmured, "Thank you. We were lucky enough to have good teachers, and we both enjoy music."

"You must go to the opera in London during the Season."

"I would like to."

"Then you have been enjoying your time in Town?"

"Of course."

Mrs. Reddington smiled, though her eyes were like those of a cat playing with its prey. "You will do well. You are pretty and original. And it does no harm to have caught Calton's eye."

"As to that, I—"

"Hush child. As long as it is only his eye, he can only do you good. But I daresay your aunt has already warned you against him. Enjoy his attentions while they last, Miss Josephine, for he is a fickle man and has stated often enough that he has no intention of marrying."

Josephine lifted her chin. "*I do not look to marry him.*"

Mrs. Reddington paused, as though suspecting the ambiguity in her remark. Something more than surprise flashed in her eyes before the smile came back. "Good. For he has some nasty habits he will never give up."

"I have no interest in nasty habits and must bow to your greater knowledge. You will excuse me? My sister is beckoning."

As she went to join Helena, Josephine wanted to fan herself, just to cool her anger. How dare the woman talk to her like that? How dare she traduce Calton like that?

Because she knows him in ways I never will.

The thought was lowering, until another, much more elevating, sprang unexpectedly into her mind. *Because she is jealous. She sees me as a threat.*

Perhaps he was as aware as she that their closeness over dinner had been noted, for when the gentlemen rejoined them in the drawing room, he did not approach her. Neither did Gough, which had been her major fear. She wondered if Calton had said something to him, and if so, what?

Tea was served but the only entertainment was the odd game of cards, in which Calton joined. Only as Aunt Darling shepherded her nieces from the room in the wake of several others, did he appear to notice her. He glanced up as they walked past his card table and caught her eye. His smile was both spontaneous and melting, and it stayed with her as she went up to bed.

Later, lying in the darkness, she thought seriously about finding her way to the library again. Just in case Calton was there. The very idea ignited her body into memory and new desire. Of course, she could not look for him again, or she would become the woman Gough already believed her to be. And she would die rather than have Calton think she was hunting him.

And yet I am, she thought in a sudden flurry of self-knowledge. *Perhaps I will wait just another half hour and then...*

"HE WARNED ME off!" Gough fumed. "How dare he?"

Selina, lying alluringly in bed while Gough paced, sighed and gave into the inevitable. "What exactly did he say?"

"Oh, amiable as you please, he told me he was a friend of the Darlings and the Blackwells and that he would always take any threat, insult, or offense against them very seriously."

Selina sat up. "Did he, indeed?" she said slowly. Did she need to be worried by this flirtation after all? She was already concerned enough to have warned the girl off, though that had hardly gone down quite as expected. Insolent chit. "Was he threatening to call you out? Just because you spoke to her on the staircase?"

"She is a flighty little thing. I might have upset her."

"You were clumsy," Selina guessed. Really, decent allies were hard to find these days. Whether or not she got Calton back—and no lover had ever made her feel as good—she wasn't sure she could bear much more of Cyril Gough. Mind you, she had underestimated the girl herself and handled her badly. So, there was only one way to take her out of Selina's way. "Ignore her. Go to the father. Offer marriage, now. When it comes to arranging settlements is time enough to state your financial requirements. Secure the engagement quickly."

"And if either of them refuses?"

"Why would they? The girl is enceinte, and she needs a husband immediately. Calton won't marry her." At least she hoped to God he wouldn't. Marriage to another wouldn't necessarily keep him from other women's beds, but she could not bear that girl to have what Selina herself could not.

Gough sat on the bed, tugging off his cravat in a thoughtful kind of way. He began to smile. "Damn me, you're right," he said, springing to his feet. He all but tore off his breeches and fell upon her in sudden and ungentle passion. She was happy enough to let him have his way, provided he did as she bade him, though she did miss the finesse of a considerate lover. Like Calton, who could give as well as take. And who never muttered another woman's name as he reached for his pleasure in her body.

JOSEPHINE DID NOT know whether to be glad or relieved when she woke up the next morning. Clearly, she had fallen asleep before she could commit the folly of scouring the house at night in search of Lord Calton.

The thought made her giggle, for no matter how shocking her new desires and behavior, a deep, warm happiness was glowing within her that had all to do with *him*. And they were under the same roof.

These pleasurable feelings lasted through breakfast and a lively walk with Helena, Talley, Calton, and the Sayles. Although she had no time alone with Calton, just being in his company along with friends was another new delight. By the time they returned to the house, where all was in preparation for the evening's ball, more guests had arrived who would stay overnight. Making her way through mountains of baggage, footmen, maids, and valets, Josephine's attention was caught by her father, beckoning her from one of the ground floor reception rooms.

She changed direction to meet him and preceded him into the room. He followed and closed the door, giving them sudden, blessed quiet.

"Is something wrong?" she asked, somewhat surprised since she could count on one hand the number of times her father had summoned her for a private meeting. If he had something to impart, he generally did so during dinner or some other routine encounter.

"Oh, no." His frown smoothed and he smiled faintly. "Quite the contrary, in fact. At least, I believe so. I have just received an offer for your hand in marriage."

Her heart seemed to jump into her throat. "You have?" she managed.

He peered at her. A man used to reading the expressions and tones of his fellow diplomats, of sovereigns, and high-ranking government officials, was not so confident with his own family. "You are not as surprised as I."

Her heart seemed to be back in its proper place though it beat a quick, hard tattoo against her ribs. She felt as if she were about to explode with anticipation, with impossible happiness. "I am waiting to hear who made this offer and what was your reply."

"Mr. Gough," Papa said, still watching her. "Viscount Denzil's heir, you know."

Gough? She stared at her father aghast. "So, he told me at our first meeting. What did you answer?"

"That you were of age to make your own decision, but that I would speak to you and let him know your decision. Do you want to speak to him before you make up your mind?"

"No!"

Papa blinked. "Is this girlish nerves? Or do you not favor his suit?"

"The latter. It never entered my head he meant marriage."

"I fail to see what else he could mean to the gently bred daughter of a gentleman."

Josephine veered away from that discussion. She did not wish to be whisked home out of Calton's orbit just yet. "Well, I hope you are not set on it, Papa, for I definitely do *not* wish to marry Mr. Gough."

"Then I shall tell him your decision, and there is an end of the matter." His gaze lingered, though and he did not dismiss her. "Is there anything else you wish to tell me?"

"Such as what?"

"Anything."

"I don't believe so. Helena and I are both looking forward to the ball."

"I'm glad to hear it. She has been looking somewhat pale recently, so it's good to see her enjoying herself again."

Josephine almost spilled out her hopes of Talley, but the secrets surrounding her sister's relationship with the Frenchman were too close, and not Josephine's to tell. So, she merely agreed cordially, "It is, isn't it?" And was relieved when her father nodded dismissal.

"A WORD WITH you, Gough?"

The words, addressed to him by Mr. Blackwell, just as the guests were gathering for tea, made him smile. He even threw a wink at Selina beside him before he turned and followed Blackwell into Wenning's library, which was deserted.

"Sir?" Gough said, trying not to smirk as he closed the door and turned to face his future father-in-law.

"I wanted to tell you with all speed and in private that I have spoken to my daughter. Sadly, while she and I are both grateful for the honor you show her, she does not favor your suit."

Gough felt his jaw drop. "Does not…"

"Exactly."

Gough drew himself up to his full height, which might have been an inch taller than the older man, though somehow, he did not feel it. "And am I not owed an interview with the lady herself? Is she not possessed of respect enough to answer my honorable proposal in person?"

Without warning, the affable, slightly vague gentleman that was the usual Blackwell vanished to be replaced by an implacable stranger. "I have let my daughter choose, but she is still under my protection, sir, and she owes you nothing. I have civilly relayed both your proposal and her answer, and now I must ask you not to importune her further. Good afternoon, Mr. Gough."

Gough felt dismissed, even though it was Blackwell who walked out, leaving the door open.

Damnation. He sank down into the nearest chair, scowling. The girl was pregnant and rejected him? And the father *let* her? Of course, he could not yet know, poor fool. But still, to deny a suitor any private interview with her…

Of course.

"Calton," he uttered with loathing. The earl had been busy last night, not only warning Gough to behave around Miss Josephine but also warning the father against him. Though what could he possibly have said? Gough was a landed gentleman with an ancient name, the heir of a viscount, and Blackwell was damned lucky to receive *any* offers for his whore of a daughter.

Well, he would come back *begging* Gough to take her off his hands soon enough. For the girl herself was clearly holding out for the Earl of Calton. She didn't have the sense to know, as Selina and Gough both did, that that bird would never fly.

CHAPTER TEN

"YOU LOOK BEAUTIFUL," Josephine told her sister as their eyes met in the looking glass. Aunt Darling's maid, who had been loaned to them for half an hour, fled back to her mistress, leaving them alone.

Helena smiled a little tremulously and smoothed the skirts of her elegant blue silk ballgown with its ruffled train. "Do you think—" She broke off, shaking her head.

"Do I think Talley will find you so?" Josephine guessed, and Helena blushed.

"I have become obvious."

"It's an improvement from impenetrable and pointlessly secretive."

"I felt so confused, so…alone."

Josephine came closer behind her and threaded her fingers through her sister's. "You were never alone."

For a moment, Helena curled her fingers around Josephine's. "I know. But he didn't come, and he didn't speak, and I was ashamed and humiliated." Her smile grew dazzling. "He is going to speak to Papa tonight."

"Does he know about the baby?" Josephine asked bluntly.

Helena's smile faded. "I meant to tell him today, but there were always people around. I will find a moment tonight *before* he speaks to Papa. But I know everything will work out. For you, too, Jo."

Josephine dragged her gaze free. "I think my heart is too wayward for that," she said ruefully.

"Lord Calton is different with you. Is he the reason you turned down Mr. Gough?"

"No, Gough is the reason I turned down Mr. Gough," Josephine said lightly.

Helena stood back and examined her. "That color seems dull until *you* wear it. It catches the lights in your hair and eyes and shimmers like autumn leaves in sunlight."

Josephine laughed. "Now you are being poetic—you must be in love. Come, let us go before Darling Aunt has to come and shoo us downstairs."

The ballroom had been stunningly decorated in Lady Wenning's inimitable style, to resemble a night sky. Against a dark blue ceiling and walls, a central chandelier shone like the moon, while smaller clumps of candles winked like stars above and around the walls. Instead of filling the ballroom with hothouse flowers or potted palms, she had arranged silhouette paintings of trees against pillars and one of the walls. The effect was charming and different and curiously enchanting.

"How beautiful!" Josephine said to her hostess as she and Helena followed Papa and Aunt Darling into the ballroom.

Lady Wenning laughed. "I was about to say the same to you."

Josephine smiled and moved on. For a moment, she was disoriented by the sea of people, and could not see her family or make out anyone else she knew. And everyone seemed to be looking at her. A flush of embarrassment spread up from her toes. She forced herself to move and then, a man stepped in front of her.

"Miss Josephine. May I have the pleasure?"

Calton, handsome as ever and carelessly distinguished in severe black and white evening dress, leavened only by the red and gold splash of his waistcoat. She took his arm from sheer instinct and relief. "Pleasure of what?"

His eyes twinkled. "The first dance. To begin with. You seem a little…discomposed."

"Everyone was staring at me," she confided. "You would tell me if my gown was torn, or I have somehow acquired a smut on my nose? Or is some rumor circulating—"

"Josephine. They are staring because you look beautiful, even more so than usual."

She cast him a dubious glance that made him laugh. "Sorry," she mumbled. "I don't really like crowds. When we were in Vienna, I learned to tolerate them by sticking close to Helena for the first quarter of an hour until I was used to all the people, and then it was easier."

"Then it was particularly brave of you to risk the ball at Maida where you knew no one."

"That was different. I was masked, and I had an important task to carry out. Besides, I hovered around the edges of the dance floor until I saw you. It was helpful, though quite arrogant of you, to disdain the mask."

"It made my face itch. Is this an acceptance of my hand for the waltz?"

She realized the orchestra was playing the introduction. To open proceedings, Lady Wenning took to the floor with the handsome young Duke of Dearham, as the highest-ranking guest in attendance, Lord Wenning with the duchess.

"Oh, yes, of course." Goodness, she had almost forgotten how her body reacted to his nearness. The strength of his arm at her waist, the light yet almost caressing clasp of his hand, the grace of his guiding movements… Feeling swamped her, almost equal parts pleasure and pain—pain because she could never have what she truly wanted.

"Has Gough bothered you any further?" he murmured.

"Not as such, though he did make an offer for me to my father."

Calton's brow tugged downward. "Did he, by God?"

"You needn't sound quite so astonished."

His frown smoothed into laughter lines. "I never attributed such good sense to him. What answer did Mr. Blackwell give him?"

"Mine."

"Ah. Perhaps that is why he has suddenly decided to depart immediately after the ball."

"Has he?" she asked with hope, for in truth the man made her uncomfortable, and she hated to feel his gaze on her. Which it often seemed to be.

"According to Wenning." Calton's gaze moved beyond her. "Your sister is dancing with Talley."

"I have cause for hope there." Hope that would mean Calton's work was done and he could leave for France as he wanted. She banished the thought and summoned a smile.

"Then why do you look so sad?" he asked softly.

She stiffened. "I don't. I am not remotely sad."

He stepped forward, turning her with just a little too much ebullience. "Then smile as only you can, for there is nothing wrong with this moment. Nothing at all."

He was right, of course. More than that, it felt suddenly perfect, something to hold on to, perhaps, through subsequent years of loneliness, but for now, everything really was…wonderful.

"Save me the supper dance, too," he murmured.

"Are you trying to make me fashionable?" she teased.

"Trying to provide us with opportunities for escape," he replied as the music came to a close and he bowed, placing her hand on his arm and strolling with her in search of Aunt Darling while her heart beat and beat with fresh excitement.

The next couple of hours fled by. The whole evening seemed somehow brightened by a new sense of hope and fun. And yet every dance, every conversation, however interesting or amusing, was in some way just a means of reaching the supper dance.

She barely thought of Gough, except when she noticed him dancing or wandering into the card room. To her relief, despite his one-time request for a dance, he seemed to have taken her father's instructions to heart and did not come near her. Or perhaps he had just forgotten and moved on.

Would Lord Calton forget, too?

When the time came for the supper waltz, she was with her sister, and Talley appeared to claim Helena, who seemed tired but happy.

"We'll save you seats at our table," Helena promised her as she glided off on Talley's arm, leaving Josephine alone to insist to an unexpected crowd of young men that she was already promised for this dance. As her crowd thinned, she just hoped Calton would remember or she would look and feel very foolish trailing after Aunt Darling and the dowagers instead.

But then, he was there, bowing over her hand, and as he led her onto the dance floor, she felt as if she were floating. Was this really all it took to be happy? Her hand in his, his attention focused on her?

She shivered with awareness as his arm touched her waist and his eyes grew...hungry.

"You are not saying anything," she observed, her voice curiously breathless.

"Neither are you. Perhaps we are both thinking of the escape I mentioned."

"What exactly did you mean?"

"Going somewhere alone, to talk." His eyes glinted as he waltzed her backward. "And I very much want to kiss you."

Heat flooded her body, not just at his words but at the raw huskiness in his voice. "Then perhaps escaping is not such a good idea."

His lips quirked. "We could begin with the talking and see how you feel."

"Are you...are you trying to seduce me?" she asked warily.

A blaze of laughter flashed across his face and was gone. "That, too, is optional. I suspect it depends on the talk."

"What are we to talk about?"

"You. Happiness. Will you come? Just for as long as you wish to."

"People will notice."

"Not if we look as if we are going early to the supper room. There is a door into the garden from there."

"You have done this before, haven't you?" She didn't know if she was amused or desolate. "Enticed women from ballrooms."

"Not to talk," he said ruefully. "I have a past you needn't listen too hard to hear about. But we have trusted each other this far, have we not?"

"Yes," she admitted, losing herself once more in his eyes, in his scent, and the sheer pleasure of his nearness. "Yes, we have."

He did not rush her. He gave her time to think. Only with every passing second, she slipped further under his spell, or perhaps under her own simple curiosity. After a few minutes, they twirled around the edge of the dance floor.

"Shall we?" he murmured, and she stopped dancing before she realized she had already decided.

He drew her aside, placed her hand on his arm once more, and they walked down the steps to the supper room. A few of the dowagers were there already. Josephine could hear their voices, but before she could see them, Calton tugged her to the left and down a narrow passage that led to the kitchen, judging by the crashing of pots and pans and shouted instructions in the distance. Well, before they got there, before they had seen more than a footman with a loaded tray, Calton pushed open a door and whisked her outside.

After the heat in the ballroom, and her own thundering excitement, the cool autumn air was welcome. She breathed it in somewhat shakily. This part of the garden was not lit. Only the terrace around the ballroom and the paths to one particularly pretty area of the formal garden were illuminated by lanterns and torches.

"The maze?" he murmured.

"If you like."

His teeth flashed white, and then they were running silently, hand-in-hand across the grass, away from the ballroom and into the deeper darkness of the maze. Only, it wasn't really so dark, for the moon was bright.

They slowed to a walk, and she gazed up at the twinkling sky. "Look, it's imitating the ballroom."

He laughed softly, keeping hold of her hand. "Grace will be thrilled to hear you say so."

She glanced at him. "How come you know this place so well?"

"I came here often as a boy. We had a lot in common, Wenning and I, both inheriting earldoms at unfeasibly young ages. He was precocious and quickly channeled all his energies into serious pursuit of diplomacy. I channeled mine into pleasure."

"Just pleasure?"

His smile was twisted. "There is no *just* about pleasure. For what it's worth, I found it in more than women, wine, and gaming. I liked my estates to be well run and my people prosperous. I liked to learn as I traveled."

"You speak in the past tense," she pointed out.

"Perhaps because recently, I have found my-self...discontented with my pleasures."

"In what way?"

"In a bored, weary, what-the-devil-am-I-doing-wasting-my-life kind of way."

"And that is why you are going abroad," she guessed, rubbing distractedly at a pain in her heart.

His eyes followed the movement of her hand. "It is why I was considering it until I encountered a bold, masked seductress who taught me many things."

Her breath caught. "Such as what?"

He brought them to a halt and raised their joined hands to his lips. He kissed her knuckles. "Such as the knowledge that I cannot run from loneliness. That the old lore of happiness from love is not necessarily lies. That making you happy could make me happy."

Her heart thudded. "M-m-me?"

"Only you," he whispered. His free hand came up and cupped her cheek. "Will you marry me, Josephine Blackwell?"

Her mouth opened to speak but no words came out. His lips brushed against it. "Will you? Please."

Tiny kisses peppered the corner of her mouth, arousing, seductive.

She swallowed. "But you do not wish to be married. You told me yourself. Even Aunt Darling says so, because of your brother."

He paused for the space of a heartbeat. Or several, considering the pace of her own. "Francis," he said. "She told you about Francis?"

"She said he was…different. That he died young from that differentness, as had one of your uncles, and that was why…"

"He was a child who never grew up. The sweetest-natured, most loving child you will ever meet. At the age of twelve, he still spoke and played like a four-year-old. But he was my brother and I loved him. And they let him die without me. They left me at school so as not to upset me. He would have missed me, he would have been frightened without me." He seemed to break off the torrent of words with a mighty effort. "Perhaps. I will never know."

She put her arms around him, instinctively comforting, and after a second, he held her close against him.

"The general belief of the doctors was that his condition ran in the family," he said, his words muffled in her hair.

"So, you would not risk fathering a child like your brother."

He drew back a little to meet her gaze. "I would not risk the pain of losing a child like my brother. But I was wrong. That was something else you taught me, without words. My selfishness. I had forgotten the lives enriched by him, mine most of all. But life *is* risk and pain. Without it, there is no happiness. Only the boredom and self-weariness that was tearing me apart. Before you and your wild schemes and your care for your sister."

She closed her eyes in despair, pressing her cheek to his. "You cannot base a marriage on such foundations. I am not a crutch. But if I have helped to open your eyes, go and live your life."

Something shuddered through him. Laughter? "Oh, my sweet, those are not the foundations I had in mind, merely another reason to love you. I want you in my life and in my bed."

His rough cheek moved against hers. His mouth hovered over her lips. His fingers found the tears she tried so hard to hide.

"You know better than anyone," she whispered, "you can have those things without marriage."

"*You* cannot."

"No," she said sadly. "And I cannot live with infidelity."

His lips brushed hers, his breath warm with a hint of wine. "I would keep my vows. With you, I would have no reason to break them."

She tried to laugh. "Oh, my dear, you would…"

"I would not. I want to be your husband, the father of your children. Tell me you want to be my wife." His mouth closed on hers with such aching tenderness that the tears came faster. "Have we not agreed that risk can be necessary to happiness?" Another kiss, deeper, more sensual than the last. Her fingers trembled as they clung to his face, his nape. "Take this chance, Josephine. For both of us. Marry me."

She caught his face between her hands when he would have taken her mouth once more. "One night and you would forget me."

His eyes glowed, with need, hot and urgent. He hauled her against his hips to leave her in no doubt of his desire and moved against her. "Is that an offer?"

"Yes." *Oh, dear God, did I really say that?*

"It might prove the truth to you," he allowed, just a little breathless. "On the other hand, it's also how your sister—"

"Don't," she pleaded.

"I won't take you without marriage. I already proved that to myself if not to you." He did not sound remotely offended.

Instead, his hands were stroking her rear, running over her hips, and upward to her breasts. His fingers massaged her nape, so arousing that she could not be still. His breath stirred her hair. His lips brushed against her ear, melting her. "But I could show you a little pleasure, a little taste of what we would miss without marriage."

Trust. Trust made her lift her face in a mute plea for that taste, for his kisses and caresses. But unexpectedly, he spun her around, her back to his chest, and she gasped as he grazed his teeth along her nape, kissing and gently nipping. One arm across her body held her to him, while he cupped her breast. His other hand stroked over her stomach, and she felt an insane urge to push upward against it.

In something like desperation, she twisted her face up, to see his face, to *ask*, but he bent his neck and kissed her mouth, and she was lost all over again. Sensation bombarded her, from his kiss, from his fingers, which somehow had found the naked skin of her breast, from the hard column pressing against her rear. Her whole body seemed to be in flames, her breath coming in short, erratic pants between kisses. The hand on her stomach stroked lower, over and over until she came to understand where the core of her desire, of her pleasure, lay. She barely even noticed when he began gently, gradually, to tug upward the fabric of her gown and her petticoat.

"I want your naked skin," he whispered in her ear, his fingers rolling her aching nipple. "All of your naked skin. But I will settle for a little. Just now…"

He shifted, inserting his knee between hers, and his hand smoothed the fine, gauze-like lawn of her chemise over her thigh and between her parted legs. A tiny moan escaped her trembling lips as her head fell back against his shoulder. Instinct made her move against his fingers, relieving the strange ache, reaching for the sweet, wild sensations flooding her. And suddenly they all coalesced into one blinding, stunning pleasure, convulsing her in waves of it.

She reached up with both hands, twisting her neck to find his mouth and gasping her bliss into his kiss.

"Marry me," he whispered against her mouth. "Love me. Trust me. Marry me."

"I do," she gasped, and even through the pleasure that seemed to go on and on, she felt him smile. She touched his cheek, felt their lips slide apart. "I will…"

She turned in his arms, throwing both arms around his neck and clinging to him. "I loved you before. From the beginning."

"I suspect I did, too, but it took me a while to realize it."

"Not that long," she said in his throat. "We've hardly known each other any length of time. We must be mad."

"If so, I like it better than sanity."

She kissed his damp skin. "So do I."

"Then I will speak to your father in the morning, though I might have to bundle Talley out of the way first."

CHAPTER ELEVEN

C ALTON HAD NOT set out to win her by wickedness. He had intended a respectful declaration, along with, perhaps, a few relatively chaste kisses and reasoned argument where necessary. But nothing with Josephine ever went to plan. However, the blinding rightness of his instinctive actions was clear in her acceptance. And in her sheer, wondering joy at this discovery of passion.

His triumph might have been mitigated by his own ferocious frustration, and God knew, he was sorely tempted to take her on the lush green grass beneath their feet. She would welcome that, too. But it seemed he was still a gentleman and he had thrown enough at her for one night. There would be other nights, endless nights and days of pleasure.

She loves me.

And that was enough for him.

For now.

He shifted position against the hedge behind him, and gently eased her garments back over her naked breast. His blood clamored to see her completely naked in candlelight and sunlight, but that, too, was for other days, other nights.

For now, he needed to get his lust under control before they returned to the party, so he adjusted them so that he held her more against his side while their heartbeats returned to something more normal. Still, he gloried in the feel of her languid fingers in his hair, of her soft, contented body sagging against him.

"You are beautiful in the moonlight as passion takes you," he whispered in her ear, and felt rather than saw her smile.

"I don't even know your Christian name."

"No one uses it. Everyone calls me Calton."

She lifted her head, peering up at him. "I don't want to be everyone."

He met her gaze and felt laughter rise. "Then you had better invent a nickname for my given name is Aurelius. Which is why no one uses it."

"I expect you beat them until they stopped. Aurelius. I rather like it."

Oddly enough, it sounded different on her lips. Kind and mysterious and…arousing, damn it. "My father was a great admirer of the writings of Marcus Aurelius," he said a shade desperately. "So, apparently, he felt necessary to burden me with it. Fortunately, I have been Calton since I was in short coats."

Idly, he stroked her hair and made a discovery. "I have ruined your coiffure, and I suspect it's beyond my ability to repair."

"I will have to sneak back to my bedchamber, where there is also another pair of dancing slippers. I suspect these are muddy and grass-stained."

"Come, then, if we can slip back in the way we came out, you can use the servants' stairs. They will still be busy with supper."

Hand in hand once more, they found their way out of the maze and flitted across the lawn to the half-hidden door between the supper room and the kitchen. They had just made it to the staircase before two footmen bolted through the passage, but they saw no one else.

At the ground floor, he said reluctantly, "If you are seen with me now, it will do your reputation no good at all."

"Are we really engaged?" she said in a rush. "Because—"

He stopped her mouth with a quick, hard kiss. "Very much

so. I will not allow you to forget it."

She smiled, looking beautiful and happy and delectably rumpled. It took considerable willpower to let her go, but he managed it, though he watched her vanish completely around the curve in the staircase before he pushed past the baize door that led to the main entrance hall. It was reasonably well lit. He walked to the large mirror near the cloakroom and straightened his cravat. He ran his fingers through his hair and brushed a few hedge leaves from his coat. Then he continued on his way to the mostly empty ballroom where the orchestra was beginning to tune-up for the final few dances.

He strolled through the open French windows onto the terrace, in search of a group to attach himself to so that the gossipmongers wouldn't suspect he had been with Josephine all that time. This worked out quite well, and he was just enjoying an amusing if salacious story when he caught sight of Andre de Talley alone on the terrace steps.

Once the story was finished, he joined in the laughter, then wandered toward the Frenchman.

"You are looking morose," he said lightly. "Though your lady seems to smile upon you."

Talley rose with a quick smile. "Not morose. Thoughtful. My lady rather threw a whole new ingredient into the mix."

Oh-oh. "A pleasant one, I hope?"

"I...I don't honestly know. I don't want it to be the reason she marries me."

Dear God, preserve us. "What reason is there apart from love, in your case and hers?"

"None. And yet there is another."

Calton smacked him across the shoulder. "You told me you could not live without her. Don't spoil it now because you discover life is not always the fairytale you want it to be. Everything you say and do has consequences, my friend. For her as well as for you. Don't be an ass, there's a good fellow."

With that, he wandered back to his friends, who were now

ambling into the ballroom to seek their partners for the next country dance.

JOSEPHINE FULLY EXPECTED her sister to quiz her over her absence at supper. But in fact, she barely saw Helena except in the distance, dancing. Josephine did not mind. She had no idea what she could or would say, for she was totally intoxicated by what had happened in the maze.

Lord Calton—Aurelius—loved her. He was going to be her husband. And in his arms… Pure happiness flooded her so that she could not be still. She danced, she chatted, and she laughed with other people while her heart was so full, she thought it would burst. In fact, so absorbed was she in her own secret joy that it took her until the last dance to notice Helena's.

Her sister looked to be enjoying herself. She smiled and danced with unflagging energy, even though she must have needed her rest. But now that Josephine actually saw her, waltzing past in the arms of a stranger, that brittle edge had returned to Helena's gaiety. Her smile was too bright, her pleasure too determined.

"Is Helena well?" she asked Talley, with whom she was enjoying the last dance.

"As you see," he replied dryly.

"I do see," she said with a hint of grimness. "Have you and she quarreled?"

"Of course not."

Josephine dragged her gaze back to him and looked into his eyes—stunned, oddly tortured eyes. "She told you."

His eyes closed briefly. "Did everyone know but me?"

"Since you didn't trouble to find out."

Talley flushed. "It shouldn't… I didn't… There are matters I cannot discuss with you," he finished in a rush. "Suffice it to say, I was surprised. And now I am to be married to save face."

She stared at him and drew nearer. "Talley, if my hands were not occupied, I would hit you. How dare you speak so? Even think so?"

"She only told me after I proposed," he said miserably.

"So that she would not *compel* you by it! Dear God, if ever I met such a pair of widgeons. Are you really so self-absorbed that you cannot see her silence speaks of her selfless love? So imbecilic that you would *blame* her for this? Two of you created this situation, and of the two, *you* are by far the more experienced. She has tried to keep mere honor out of it, so that love has its chance. I am disappointed to find you are not so brave or so constant."

Her words tumbled out with low intensity, inaudible to any but him. His eyes widened, darkened with something like shame and guilt, so she pushed her point. "Do you have any idea what she has gone through to avoid compelling you? To be sure you loved her?"

"I… Please stop talking about it. People are looking at us."

"Don't want any talk, Talley?"

"That is unkind of you and unfair."

"I do hope so."

He regarded her with frustration and a hint of amusement. "I never realized you were so formidable."

"I am. So is Helena. So, if you want to be part of her life, stop being an ass."

An arrested look came into his eyes, and she hoped she had finally made an impression, for she had had more than enough of tiptoeing around his feelings. Calton had shown Helena more concern than her lover.

Calton…

She smiled because she could not help it, which seemed to startle Talley, but fortunately, the dance came to an end, as did the ball. Talley left her with her father, seeming in a hurry to be somewhere else—hopefully with Helena.

But in truth, anxieties over her sister had slipped well behind her flowering love for Lord Calton and his even more astonishing love for her. Marriage with *him*, a lifetime with him and his intoxicating kisses, and that wild, overwhelming pleasure…

She saw him only once as she joined the throng heading upstairs to bed. Somehow, he was beside her, presenting her with a night candle, making sure their fingers touched. And when her gaze flew up to his, a smile trembling on her lips, his eyes smiled back.

"Tomorrow," he murmured, and that was all. From halfway up the staircase, she saw him vanishing into the billiard room with several other men.

In something of a dream, she made her slow way up the rest of the stairs and along the passage to her bedchamber. Although tired, she didn't see how she would ever sleep. She felt strange, as if she were floating, disembodied, someone else entirely. And yet at the same time, she had never been so glad to be Josephine Blackwell, because Calton loved her. Because, against the odds, she made Calton happy.

By the light of a solitary lamp in her bedchamber, she saw that Helena was already in bed, although from her breathing she was not yet asleep.

"You must be exhausted, poor thing," Josephine said softly. "How did you get out of your ballgown?"

"I seized an early opportunity with Darling Aunt's Bolton."

Josephine sat on the side of her sister's bed and presented her back. "Do you have the energy to…?"

Helena sat up, and Josephine glanced over her shoulder. Even in the dim light, it was clear her sister had been crying. Josephine faced forward while Helena unhooked the gown and unlaced her stays with more speed than care before dropping back onto the bed and turning her back.

Josephine gazed at her unmoving figure for a moment, then said, "I gather your revelation did not go as well as we had hoped?"

Helena hunched her shoulder in silence.

"Lena," Josephine urged.

"No, it did not," Helena snapped. "He thought I was marrying him only because I am with child."

"I'm sure he does not really think that. You have had weeks to come to terms with this. He is only just beginning."

"I do not have weeks for him to forgive me! I shall have to go abroad after all."

"No, no, I don't believe so, Lena! Tomorrow—"

"He does not love me at all, does he?"

"Oh, he does. He would not look so tormented if he did not care. He is just an idiot male making adjustments to your pedestal—and his own."

"You sympathize with him," Helena accused.

"I am trying to understand him."

Helen jerked her head around, staring at her. "Do you love him, too? You would not take him from me, would you, Jo?"

Josephine blinked. "Why *the devil* would you think that?"

"Don't swear," Helena said loftily. "I saw the way you were talking to him during the last waltz, the way you smiled at him."

Josephine jumped to her feet. "Oh, for the love of… Trust me, if I smiled at him during the last waltz, I was thinking of something else entirely!" She took a deep breath. "Go to sleep, Helena. Tomorrow, everything will be better."

Helena did not move or reply. Josephine paced to the window and sank onto the embrasure seat without removing her clothes. She was fairly sure the situation between Helena and Talley would resolve itself in the light of day when Talley had had the chance to think and come to his senses.

In any case, there was nothing she could do for them tonight, and all she really wanted to do was remember her dances with Calton, to go over every word they had exchanged, and relive every kiss and embrace and…*that.*

She was not blind to the fact that despite his obvious delight, even triumph, in the bliss he had given her, it had been a one-sided pleasure. Which was odd, because from all she had ever heard, it was meant to be the other way around.

Perhaps I am wanton.

And perhaps there was a lot more to come. More than anything, she wanted to give him the same bliss he had given her. Only she didn't know how.

She had a good deal to learn, and the thought of it made her smile into the darkness. The house had grown quiet, and the lights on the grounds below were all extinguished. Reaching up, she opened the window a narrow crack to let in some fresh air.

Some activity was still going on in the distance. Low voices, the faint clop of horses' hooves in the gravel, the trundling of carriage wheels. Mr. Gough, probably, making his departure. Which made tomorrow just about perfect.

She touched her lips in wonder.

Helena made a huffing noise in her slumbers. If Josephine did not sleep now, she would never be ready for tomorrow.

It is already tomorrow.

A scratch sounded at the bedchamber door, so unexpected that she merely stared toward it without moving. It came again.

Calton. She rose, snatching up the nearest shawl and flinging it around her shoulders to hide her unfastened state. She blushed, tingling all over to remember what he had seen and touched in the maze.

Trying to breathe normally, she opened the door. A man with a single candle stood there. But it was not Calton. He was older, shorter, well but plainly dressed and when he bowed, it was with the oddly superior servility of a gentleman's valet. He held out a folded paper to her, bearing her name.

Calton's valet. With a quick smile, she took the note and closed the door.

I cannot wait. Come to the stables, I beg you. C.

Wretch, she thought, catching her breath on a laugh. But at least he begged, and that was not characteristic. Moving as quietly as she could, she took her warm traveling cloak from the wardrobe, slipped on her comfortable half-boots, grabbed a reticule from habit, and left, relighting her night candle and dousing the lamp as she went.

Hurrying along the now dark passage and down the stairs by her solitary candlelight, she wondered what was so urgent. Was it to do with Helena and Talley? Or just with *them*? Her stomach twisted in anticipation.

But why the stables? Just because it was far enough away from the house? And it would be quiet with Gough gone…

He would not want to elope, would he? He must know her father would raise no objections to the match. No, it was either a private discussion or an assignation, either of which was fine by Josephine.

Even the hall was in darkness. The servants and the billiard room party must already have retired. She turned the huge key in the front door, quietly pulled back the bolts, and opened it. An unlit lantern stood on the front step, so she lit it from her candle before lifting it and leaving the candle in its place.

She closed the door right over without letting the latch click and hurried down the path to the stables. Emerging through the overhanging trees, she saw a traveling carriage with matched greys in the traces, pointing toward the main drive. For the first time, a hint of unease passed through her, making her pause, because if this was Gough's coach, she wanted to be nowhere near it.

On the other hand, it could equally be Calton's vehicle. If he had been called away suddenly, it would explain his urgency, although that didn't quite fit with the terse message he had sent via his valet.

She edged around the trees, noticing that the coachman was already in place, that bags had been strapped to the back of the vehicle and its lanterns were lit for traveling in the dark. A furtive glance showed her that the carriage itself was empty. But then, surely it would be driven up to the house to collect the traveler.

She slipped past it to the door of the stables, which were in darkness. Within, all was quiet save for an equine snort and the faint shifting of a horse's hooves.

Something was not right. She gripped the lantern tighter. "My lord?"

A shadow moved within the deeper darkness and resolved into a man.

"Miss Blackwell," said Cyril Gough. "I am glad to see you so punctual. Shall we?"

He moved with speed, taking advantage of her surprise to grasp her arm in a frighteningly strong grip that she could not shake off though she tried vigorously. As he began to drag her toward the carriage, she swung the lantern at him, opening her mouth to scream at the same time.

A rough hand clamped over her mouth from behind, and another seized her wrist, snatching the lantern before it could get anywhere near Gough's head. She bit the hand over her mouth, hard, eliciting only a snarl and no relaxing of the suffocating grip. Despite her furious wriggling and kicking, she was thrown inside the coach, which took off even before the door was closed.

She was hauled upright and realized she was squashed between two men—Gough and the man who had delivered the message. Not Calton's valet, but Gough's.

CHAPTER TWELVE

ANDRE DE TALLEY knew he had no chance of sleep, so he had slipped out of a side door, taking the key with him. He needed to walk off the fog clouding his mind and think clearly, for Helena's news of her pregnancy had hit him like a bombshell.

He didn't know why, for it had always been a risk since that crazy moment in Brighton. Even then, insane with love and lust as he had been, he had retained enough sense to withdraw, as he thought, before the crucial moment. And when they had met again in London, she had treated him as though he were of no account. And although they had now relaxed once more into their old relationship—without him taking advantage of her this time—she had been so merry and Helena-like that it had never entered his head she was with child.

He set off across the lawn without much care for where he was going. Through his confusion and hurt, he had almost said to her, "Is it mine?" Thank God he had not sunk so low, for he knew the child was his, and yet that she had kept it from him, that she had only turned to him once she had realized her condition…

But even that was not necessarily true. He had been so caught up in his new post in London, ensuring he could stay there in order to be close to Helena, that he had lost track of the time and of Helena herself, who must have felt abandoned. That was his shame, along with taking advantage of her in the first place.

And now…now, God knew what she was feeling. That he had abandoned her all over again. Lord Calton had tried to tell him. Josephine had been more brutal. But they both made sense. And that was his third shame.

If he walked away now, if he didn't go to her immediately, he would lose her. And that, *that* was the unbearable, unthinkable thing in all of this. Helena was his to look after, his beloved and the mother of his child. He stopped dead and looked about him.

He didn't think he had come far. There were the stables over there, with a carriage outside—Gough going on his way as threatened. He seemed to be an unsavory person, and he would not be missed.

As Talley strode down the track back toward the house, another lantern caught his attention, carried by a female figure in a traveling cloak.

Something familiar in her movement caused him to quicken his step toward her, but she was edging around the wood now, past the carriage, and he could not see her.

And then, in a clatter of hooves and wheels, the carriage almost mowed him down. He fell back against the bushes, glaring at the carriage, and clear as day through the side window, he saw two men and the frightened, furious face of Josephine Blackwell.

He did not stop to think but threw himself onward to the stables, and with all speed, saddled the horse Calton had lent him. He could not take time to raise the alarm at the house, but in the hope his gesture would be understood, he hastily tied his embroidered handkerchief to the bench beside the stable building and galloped off in pursuit of the carriage.

Josephine stared from one captor to the other, breathing deeply. "I don't know what you hope to achieve by abducting me, but unless your goal is suffocation, one of you will have to move."

Gough's expression shifted from wary to admiring. He flicked a glance at his henchman who, with apparent reluctance, moved to the opposite bench. Josephine immediately put as much distance as possible between herself and Gough.

"So, what do you want?" she demanded coldly.

Gough smiled. "You, my dear."

"I believe you have already had this discussion with my father."

"But not with you."

"I'm sure my father passed on the gist of my reply," she said scathingly.

"Well, we shall have several hours to convince you to change your mind, which as we all know is a lady's privilege."

"I won't change my mind. Now stop being ridiculous and make this coach stop *at once*."

Gough sat back, regarding her with fascination and absolutely no alarm. "You really do think Calton will offer for you?"

She lifted a brow, maintaining haughty silence.

"Even now?" he went on, "when you have just eloped with another man while bearing the child of *yet another* man?"

Josephine blinked, distracted from her instinctive denial of elopement by his last accusation. "*What?*"

"I did wonder for a while if the child were Calton's, but Selina Reddington assures me it is unlikely. And besides, I don't think you've known him long enough. But even if he is helping you, his intentions do not include marriage to a fallen woman."

"But to be clear," she said frowning, "you believe yours do?"

"Probably. Depending on your—er...pre-marital performance. I don't *need* the Darling money, but there's no denying it would help. And after said premarital performance, to say nothing of the baby, I shall be well able to dictate settlements to your charming papa."

"My father will shoot you." Only as she said the words with ineffable contempt, did she realize what she was clutching on her lap, hard between her white fingers. Inside the reticule she had grabbed from her bedchamber, she could feel the outline of the little gold-mounted pistol with which she had once threatened Calton. It was not yet loaded, of course, but if she could find a moment…

"Shoot the only man willing to marry you and save you from shame?" he mocked.

"You abducted me," she retorted. "The shame is yours."

He smiled. "And the child?"

She laughed. "What child? I am no more enceinte than you are." She jumped up to batter on the coach roof for the vehicle to stop.

Gough yanked her back down before she could touch it. "It will make no difference. My coachman is deaf and blind when he has to be."

"I think you might find he talks a great deal when the alternative is the hangman's noose. Abduction *is* a hanging offense, you know."

"You forget, I have your shame to shut your father's mouth."

"Are we back to that again? You are a complete fool."

He scowled as though her insult actually stung. "Am I? I heard you, Miss Josephine, at the ruin, in conversation with Calton."

She curled her lip. "Eavesdropping is clearly not an infallible way to the truth."

Gough's henchman let out an exclamation. She followed his gaze to the window where a horseman was galloping alongside the carriage.

Talley?

CALTON, SITTING ON the back terrace steps, thought he should probably go inside soon. It was cold and quiet, and dawn was still an hour or so off. He heard the distant sounds of carriage wheels and horses on the drive—presumably Gough leaving, which was all to the good.

Yes, he should go inside and get some sleep before bearding Josephine's father. Before seeing her again. Before luring her to somewhere private and secluded and indulging…

Don't think of indulgence, he told himself severely, *or there will be no sleep at all.*

A swishing movement behind him forced him to his feet. For a delicious moment, he thought he beheld Josephine in her night attire, come to offer him his heart's desire. But no, it was Helena who stood before him, more beautiful than his beloved if one looked dispassionately, and yet somehow paler, less vital. At least to Calton.

He bowed in silence, but she did not return the courtesy.

"Where is my sister?" she blurted.

A sharp pang of unease pierced his happiness. "You share a chamber, do you not?"

"She is not in her bed. We… I said some unkind things to her. I thought she might have come outside—I heard a door close, though I suppose that could have been you."

There was no real reason for his feeling of dread, and yet he could not forget that he had just heard Gough's coach leave Harcourt. Had there not been hoofbeats after that, too? Altogether, far too many people seemed to be abroad.

"Look in the library," he said briskly. "And back in your own room. I'll search around the other rooms and meet you back here in five minutes."

She nodded and scuttled off inside. He closed the French doors behind them. He would rather have gone to the stables first, but he had no wish to alarm Helena. Instead, he went toward his own chamber, listening briefly at several doors on the way to see if any of his trusted friends were awake. Only at Talley's, which was in silence, did he then open the door into darkness.

"Talley, are you asleep? I think I might need you to…" He held his candle high, which showed him the bed was empty.

Indeed, it had not been slept in. Talley was not here. He swung around and left, hurrying now directly to the front door, which was unbolted and not even properly closed.

Swearing beneath his breath, he ran around to the stables. A still glowing lantern had been abandoned at the stables' main door. Calton picked it up and looked inside. All the stalls were full of guests' carriage horses and several extra riding horses, too. On impulse, he went to his own and drew in a shuddering breath.

Then quick footsteps outside had him striding for the door.

Helena Blackwell stood in a traveling cloak by a wooden bench to the side, gazing at an embroidered handkerchief that seemed to have been tied around its arm.

"That is Andre de Talley's," she said in a flat voice. "Josephine has taken her cloak and reticule."

"De Talley is not in his room," Calton observed. "And I suspect he has taken my horse."

"They are together," she whispered, sinking onto the bench. "I knew it!"

"What are you imagining?" Calton said harshly. "That they have eloped together? Why would Talley then leave us a token?" He flung his hand toward the handkerchief and strode back into the stables, to lead out his remaining horse for saddling and bridling.

"Then what is he doing?" Helena demanded.

"Looking after your sister, I suspect," he said grimly, tightening the girths. "Which is my task."

"Is it?" she said with interest, and then, springing to her feet. "I'll come with you."

"No, wait here and cover for her if necessary. I'll be faster alone. But don't fret, they cannot have gone far."

As THE HORSES slowed to a standstill, Gough swore and wrenched down the window. "Get these horses moving at once or—"

"Good morning," Talley's voice said amiably. He appeared at the window, looping very long reins around a tree at the side of the road. Clearly, the coachman had given him no fight, and he did not appear to be armed.

"Have you taken to highway robbery, monsieur? Having lost the damned war?"

"Diplomacy, *monsieur*," Talley replied. "For now. Come down, if you please." To help, he wrenched the door from Gough's hands and let down the steps. "Both gentlemen, if I may call you that, first."

"I have no intention of leaving my own carriage at the orders of a dashed Frenchman!"

"Think again, sir," Josephine said, for during the distraction of her companions, her hands had been busy extracting the pistol from her reticule, and it now pointed straight at Gough's heart.

There was a distinct pause, during which she did not dare look at Talley. Then the valet all but shoved his master out of the door and hastened down after him. Josephine followed them, keeping the pistol aimed, although she had to hold it too tightly to prevent her hand from shaking.

"I see you came prepared, Miss Jo," Talley remarked. "I should have known. Naturally, I offer my escort back to Harcourt. My only question is, what would you like to do with these two?"

"The lady is traveling with us willingly," Gough said smoothly. "More willingly than I, truth be told. I believe she thinks if she is compromised, I will marry her."

"Why would you believe that?" Talley asked, clearly amused, "when she has already turned you down?"

"That was merely her father, for, of course, he does not know."

"Know?" Talley urged, apparently fascinated.

"That the whore is already with child."

Talley took a step nearer him, his eyes flashing with fury

"You will mind your lying, common mouth!"

"I do not lie. Look at her. It's quite clear she will not shoot me!"

"I might try," Josephine said conversationally. "Although anger has made my hands a little shaky, and I am not *quite* sure what I might hit. I might, for example, aim to disable you and hit something vital instead. Mind you, any kind of wound can fester and kill you.

A wary look entered Gough's eye. He changed tack. "I think she is insane. And I suppose you must be the poor fool who fathered her unborn brat. I admit to surprise, for I thought you were mooning over the sister."

"I am."

Despite everything, Josephine beamed at him. "Are you? Then we must return to Harcourt immediately so that you can tell her so, for she has got some silly—ah!"

Distraction had cost her dearly, for she had forgotten about the damned valet again, and he had already grabbed her wrist before she could move or even heard Talley's abrupt warning.

The man wrenched the pistol from her hand and shoved her back against the coach. A horse snorted at the movement.

"Shoot him!" Gough all but screamed. "Shoot him quickly!"

Oh, the devil! Even as the unladylike curse sounded silently in her mind, the valet pulled the trigger.

A deafening silence filled the night.

"It's not loaded," Josephine said apologetically. "No ball, no powder."

Talley laughed, a shaky, not quite amused sound. "You threatened them with an unloaded pistol?"

"You came without one?" she retorted.

"Get her back in the coach," Gough snarled to the valet. "*You!*" He pointed furiously at the coachman who still sat on his box watching events unfold with apparent interest. "Untie the reins, and this time do not stop for anything!"

The coachman sighed loudly and began to climb down. As his

boot hit the road, he nodded back the way they had come. "You might want to think again, guv. Numbers piling up against you, by the looks of things. Pretty sure I know that fellow—or at least his horse."

"And he *will* have a pistol," Talley said with satisfaction. "Maybe two."

Josephine evaded the valet's suddenly indifferent grip to peer up the road. Furiously galloping hooves filled her ears as a horseman bore down upon them at frightening speed. Gough gawped, then, avoiding Talley, slid around the back of the coach to the other door. Josephine tripped him, causing him to stumble and slow, and then the rider—Lord Calton, magnificently frightening in his fury—rode straight at Gough, who let out a grunt of sheer panic.

For a moment, it looked as if Calton would ride straight into the coach, simply to get at the paralyzed Gough. Josephine held her breath while Talley yanked her well out of the way on the grass verge.

At the last possible moment, Calton's horse veered, avoiding the carriage, but the rider lashed out with one fist and sent Gough staggering, sprawling over the coach steps and half inside the vehicle. The horse slowed and turned and, before it had even halted beside Talley's, Calton had slid to the ground. He strode straight over Gough without even kicking him on the way past, only to snatch Josephine into his arms and crush her mouth beneath his.

Stunned, she could only yield, letting her arms slide around his waist to hold him, or perhaps just to hold herself upright under his thorough assault. A bizarre sense of safety and happiness flooded her, for all would be well now that *he* was here.

Even though she was alone in the middle of nowhere, at night, with five men to whom she was not related.

"Calton," Talley said quietly. "You might want to flourish that pistol about now?"

Calton released her mouth, though not the rest of her, and

she saw Gough had hauled himself to his feet, still clutching his jaw. The valet, whose stance resembled that of a pugilist in drawings she had seen, watched Calton very carefully.

Calton curled his lip. "I won't need a pistol to deal with those scoundrels. Not unless you, Gough, are still in London when I return there. Or you open your mouth even to speak the name of this lady—and trust me, I will hear if you do. And then I *will* involve pistols and I will kill you."

Gough's eyes shifted.

"Talley?" Calton inquired.

"He told his valet to shoot me," Talley mused. "If I come across either of them again, I might have to reveal that, though whether to society or to the authorities I am not yet sure."

"Both," Calton suggested. "Seems to me you had best leave the country, Gough. And rot in some quiet corner of the world where neither of us will ever fall over you."

Gough and the valet almost tripped over each other to get back into the carriage. The coachman did not hurry himself to untangle the reins and climb back up to his box.

"If you are unhappy in your work," Josephine called to him. "You might seek other employment."

He stared at her, then a quick grin dissolved his stolid features. "I'll collect my pay first. But thank you kindly for the suggestion." He tipped his hat with his whip. "Best of luck to you, ma'am, gents."

He set his horses off at a civilized pace, and Calton's mount ambled up to him. Calton released Josephine with apparent reluctance, scooped up the fallen pistol, which he pocketed, and swung himself up into the saddle before reaching down to her with one hand.

She took it, jumped, and let herself be hauled up in front of him.

"We should return to Harcourt well before anyone is up," Talley remarked from the back of his own mount.

"Miss Blackwell is up," Calton said casually, "and awaits your return."

"Is she angry with me?" Talley asked.

"I suggest you ask her. In fact, I suggest you have much still to say to each other, for her first conclusion was that you had eloped with Josephine!"

Talley blinked and muttered something in French below his breath.

"Did you think that, too?" Josephine asked Calton as the horses began to walk back along the road.

He shook his head. "No. I knew Gough was behind the whole thing."

"It was a very dashing rescue," she told him with a quick, suddenly shy smile.

His lips quirked. "Oh, I'm sure you and Talley had it all in hand without me."

Josephine sighed. "Well, we did until I forgot about the wretched valet again, and they discovered the pistol was not loaded."

"Not loaded?" He frowned at her. "But I gave you the ball back."

"I keep it separately," she said with dignity, and saw understanding dawn in his eyes.

Smiling, he lowered his head closer to hers. "With the pressed harebell, perhaps?"

"Perhaps." She hid her face against his throat and smiled against his skin, inhaling its distinctive scent before she kissed it.

"Perhaps we should move a little faster," Talley said apologetically. "I believe it might rain."

CHAPTER THIRTEEN

DAWN WAS BREAKING as they approached the stables from the woods. They dismounted and walked the horses along the path to the stables until Josephine could see her sister wrapped in a traveling cloak and a horse blanket, apparently sound asleep on the bench. Wordlessly, Josephine took the reins from Talley.

He did not even glance at her as he ran ahead to Helena and crouched down at her knees. "Helena. Helena, wake up. You will be chilled to the bone."

Her head lifted, and then with a little cry of joy, she flung her arms about him.

"Helena, my Helena," he uttered, his voice muffled. "If I loved you less, I'm sure I would handle this better. Forgive me?"

"Oh, forgive *me*, I had no idea…"

Calton tugged Josephine and the horse through the stable door to give the other two a little privacy. "In just a moment, you and Helena should go together up to the house. The staff will be allowed to sleep late but we can't rely on there being no one about."

She nodded, frowning, then said in a rush, "Gough thought I wanted you for your title. Other people will think that, too, but…you don't, do you?"

He took her into his arms. "No. There was always something between us that had nothing to do with title or rank or position. I always knew, just not what to call it." He rested his forehead against hers. "You are mine, as I am yours."

She kissed his lips, long and tenderly.

"Then you will not mind a quick and quiet wedding?" he asked huskily.

"I think I will like that."

"Good." He swooped for a quick, hard kiss. "Then go and take Helena back to the house and send Talley to help me with the horses."

⟫⟫⟨⟨

CALTON'S VALET WOKE him at the hour agreed.

Calton groaned but hauled himself into a sitting position to accept the coffee thrust into his desperate hands. "Is the household up and about?"

"The servants are clearing up, my lord, and a few of the guests are heading down to breakfast."

Calton took another gulp of coffee and threw off the bed-clothes. "Then you had better shave me and lay out the decent morning clothes. And then begin to pack. We're leaving today."

"For France, my lord?" the man asked morosely.

"No. For London."

Breakfast was a subdued meal, due, no doubt, to the previous evening's over-indulgence in many cases. Grace Wenning presided, since she was probably awake with her baby in any case, but she seemed content to eat, drink tea, and flip through a newspaper. Since there was no sign of Mr. Blackwell, Calton approached his hostess as she excused herself.

"Tell me, which room is Mr. Blackwell in?"

She told him, saying only, "Don't harass the poor man at this hour or he'll send you away with a flea in your ear."

Calton kissed her cheek and ran cheerfully upstairs to risk said flea.

127

Half an hour later, he emerged from Blackwell's bedchamber, grinning, and strode back to his own room to see how the packing progressed and to write brief notes to Josephine and Talley. Then, taking the notes with him, he went to make farewells to his host and hostess.

However, as he turned the corner of the passage, Selina Reddington emerged from her bedchamber in front of him.

"Selina," he said when she looked as if she would ignore him, and she paused, allowing him to catch up.

"My lord."

"Did you put Gough up to this mischief?"

Her wide eyes were guileless. "What mischief?"

"Trying to abduct an innocent young lady."

Selina smiled. "I hear the lady is not so innocent."

He leaned closer. "Then you heard wrongly."

"Well, she won't be now if she's with Gough," Selina drawled.

"But she is not," Calton said gently. "She is with her sister and her aunt."

She cast him a venomous glance of annoyance but said nothing.

"Which puts me in an awkward position," he said. "One I have never been in before."

"Do tell."

"One where I can no longer regard a lady with whom I have been intimate as a friend. We are not friends, Selina, and if you dare come after my wife in any way, I will bring you down. Good morning."

She would know he could do it, too, for the simple reason that his connections were better than hers, and she would only make a fool of herself playing the shunned mistress in public.

He strode past her and downstairs, in search of his host and hostess, whom he found by the morning room window with their arms around each other, her ladyship's head on her husband's shoulder.

Once, he might have made light of such marital affection. Now, it was what he ardently sought, so he said only, "Sorry to interrupt. I am making my farewells early, Grace, and ask you to deliver these notes for me. Also to keep an eye on the wellbeing of the Miss Blackwells."

"Oh dear, you are never going to the continent after all, are you?" Grace asked in flattering dismay.

"Actually, no. I have some business to take care of in Town."

JOSEPHINE WOULD HAVE thought this note purporting to come from Lord Calton was also a forgery, had it not been given to her by Lady Wenning herself. Her ladyship had bustled out of the library with a quick smile, closing the door and leaving Josephine with her father, aunt, and sister.

"Gone? He's gone to Town?" she said indignantly. *Without saying goodbye? How could he?* Hurt and doubt began to roll through her.

"You slept too long," her father said mildly. "He could leave it no later to begin his journey. But he did speak to me before he left."

Her gaze flew to his. "Did he?" Maybe it was not so bad, although…

"I gather you are in favor of a match with Lord Calton?"

She nodded, not trusting herself to speak.

He smiled faintly. "Well, you must know I have nothing against it. I like the man. I believe he will rise above his reputation and will look after you properly. And you will be a countess!"

Her eyes widened. "Oh dear, so I will."

Helena laughed. "You will have to behave and be dignified."

"So will he," Aunt Darling said darkly. "But we shall talk about that nearer the wedding. Your sister also has news."

Smiling, Josephine turned to her sister. "Talley?"

Helena laughed with sheer joy. "He also spoke to Papa this afternoon, so it seems he is to be rid of both of his daughters at once!"

"Oh, he will never really be rid of us!"

Relief and happiness for her sister mingled with her own wonder. And yet her personal feelings seemed oddly distant, almost like a play, because he was not there with her. What she felt in her bones was *longing*, rather than the obvious delight of her sister. Without Calton there, the edge of pleasure and excitement in her stay had gone, and despite all the entertainments organized by Lady Wenning, she merely drifted, smiling amiably while her heart silently yet fiercely demanded the presence of her love.

When she packed to depart two days later, she put his letter with the pressed flower and the ball that had once resided in her pistol in a reticule at the bottom of her trunk and wondered if he would come the day they arrived back in London.

Or if he had changed his mind.

Being a gentleman, he would probably still marry her, since he had asked her father for her hand. But if he did not love her, that would be worse torture than being alone.

Talley accompanied them on the journey back to London, though mostly on horseback. Josephine was glad to see her sister watching him as he rode, waiting to speak to him at every halt, to slip away for a secret kiss before retiring to their separate bedchambers. But she missed Calton. She wanted him *here*.

Trying not to dwell on her frustrations, she passed the journey mostly in reading and dozing, letting Helena's chatter about bride clothes and houses float over her.

They were actually passing Maida Pleasure Gardens before she paid much attention to the road. "This is an odd way to come into London, is it not?"

"We've arranged to stop at Renwick's Hotel for the night," her father said.

Of course, even mention of Renwick's stirred a positive hornets' nest of memories and yearnings she was not sure she wished to deal with. "But we can easily reach Aunt Darling's before dark."

"Oh, we've had enough travel for one day. I hear Renwick's is very comfortable."

But if they pressed on to Town now, she might see Calton tomorrow, or even this evening. She bit her lip, allowing that Aunt Darling and even her father, who was no longer a young man, might be in need of the rest.

The hotel was certainly expecting them, for they were greeted with huge smiles and swept off to their rooms. Which didn't seem to be as comfortable as all that. There was a bedchamber and a sitting room, but it seemed she and Helena and their aunt were all to share.

"Wash and change for tea, girls," Aunt said gaily.

Josephine sighed and went through the motions, seizing a gown at random from her trunk.

"Not that one, dear," Aunt Darling said, taking it from her and throwing it aside. She rummaged and came up with a newer and rather more becoming green muslin with a matching Paisley shawl.

The sisters exchanged amused glances, and Josephine donned the green dress. Bolton, Aunt's maid, stopped fussing with her mistress and turned her attentions to Helena's hair, and then Josephine's.

"Well, we do look rather fine for tea," Josephine murmured, half-amused. "Do we have it in public, or in the sitting room?"

"Come with me," Aunt said mischievously, "and I shall show you."

In fact, a footman was lurking in the passage, apparently with the task of guiding them to tea. Helena took Josephine's arm and they trooped after him and Aunt Darling along the passage until the footman threw open a door on their left and they walked into a pleasant, bright sitting room that seemed full of people.

Her father was there, talking to Talley and a young man she

did not know. An extraordinarily beautiful couple were laughing as they turned toward the door, and the gentleman nudged their companion, who still had his back to her. He turned and, almost like a dream, she beheld Lord Calton.

He did not seem surprised to see her, though his face lit into one of those dazzling smiles that had melted her from the beginning. Without hesitation or even an excuse to his companions, he strode toward her.

Almost in a daze, she reached one hand toward him, perhaps to prove to herself he was real and not conjured from her own pathetic longings.

"Josephine." His low, curiously hungry voice vibrated through her as he took her hand, raised it to his lips, and kissed it. "I told them to tell you, but they didn't, did they?"

"Tell me what?" she asked bewildered. "Are we not having tea?"

His eyes danced. "Not yet. If you don't dislike the idea very much, we're going to be married first."

She had the horrible feeling that she gaped. "Now?"

"Now. I came back to Town before you to arrange the special license. Licenses, plural. I thought we should share the day with your sister and Talley, considering they are responsible for our meeting. That man with your father is Lord William Gorse, a friend and ordained clergyman. And these," he added, tugging her gently toward the beautiful couple he had just left, "are my friends, Mr. and Mrs. Stephen Dornan, who have just returned from Paris, where Dornan won a most prestigious prize for his portraits. Dornan, Aline, Miss Josephine Blackwell."

She must have said the right things because they smiled at her, looking intrigued. And then Calton drew her a little apart, standing in front of her so that he blocked her from the rest of the room.

"I didn't want you ambushed like this," he said ruefully. "I wanted you to look forward to it. Your family obviously thought it would be a more delightful surprise for you."

"Even Helena knew," she said wonderingly. "The signs were there but I was too…" She flushed.

"Too what?" he asked softly.

"Distracted." She met his gaze. "I missed you."

"Do you mind this? Will you marry me now?"

And suddenly the unreality of the previous few days vanished into sheer awareness, of him, of the hugeness of the moment, and of the adventure to come. She smiled into his eyes and heard his breath catch.

"I don't mind this at all, and I would like to marry you now."

Two hours later, she returned to the hotel from a walk around the grounds with her husband. She had wanted the fresh air and exercise and needed this innocuous time alone with him to remember and grow used to him again before the looming intimacy of their new marital chamber.

All her things had been moved to his suite of rooms.

She looked around it. "Rather grander than the mere bed-chamber you had when I first encountered you here."

"I felt the occasion demanded rather more."

"Am I really the Countess of Calton?"

"As surely as I am the earl." His arm slipped loosely around her waist, and she leaned into him. They had decided to stay here for a few days and then travel not to Europe but to his estate in Suffolk, to make it their home.

Her heartbeat quickened. She said, "Do you remember the night of the ball? In the maze?"

"How could I forget it?" His lips buried themselves in her hair, dislodging several pins.

"You took me by surprise."

"In a good way, I hope."

A breathless laugh escaped her. "In a wonderful way! So

much so that it was only later I realized the…the wonder was all mine."

"Not so," he said huskily. "I had never known such pleasure as giving you that moment."

She caught his face between her hands. "Will I be able to give *you* such moments?"

"Oh, my sweet, many," he whispered, threading his fingers through her hair so that pins fell in clusters. "Many and many and…" His mouth covered hers, and the kiss was long and sweet, a tasting, and yet sensual and knowing, and, somehow, another vow.

When their lips parted at last, he took her hand and led her through the elegant sitting room to the bedchamber, where he slowly undressed her, among many soft, breathless kisses, and then let her do the same for him.

Apart from a few distant swimmers during one memorable summer in Italy, Josephine had never seen a naked adult male. The power of his raw beauty took her breath away as she slowly let her fingertips explore, from his handsome, beloved face to his broad shoulders, to the hard muscles rippling beneath the skin of his arms and chest and stomach, wherever she touched him. And then there was the strange, male organ jutting straight up, so hard beneath the velvet soft skin, and below…

When he kissed her now, there was no barrier between them, no clothes, no doubts, only a wild flaming of desire that grew and grew with his every caress. He lifted her onto the bed and climbed after her. He lay over, worshipping her breasts with his hands and mouth, constantly moving under her own exploring caresses. And then she could not be still either, and when his fingers trailed between her legs, stroking where they had before, in the maze, the same, delicious pleasure spiked through her.

He kissed her as he had then, but before she had time to worry that he still had not found such pleasure in her, she felt a very different nudge between her legs. And in wonder she opened to him, welcoming his slow entering of her body until she could not bear to be still.

"I love you, Josephine, only you, always you," he whispered.

"Only you, always you," she echoed, almost on a moan as a deeper, more intense pleasure began *inside* her, spiraling and sweeping through her until her very breathing was ecstasy. And then, at last, she watched him reach his own bliss and wept with joy because she had given it to him.

It was the first of many joys they gave each other over the years as they grew closer and more knowledgeable. Together, they looked after their people and the land that was his responsibility, and they brought up their children in an atmosphere of warmth and fun. He never did stray from the marital bed, and neither did she, for they found in each other their perfect lady and gentleman of pleasure.

About Mary Lancaster

Mary Lancaster lives in Scotland with her husband, three mostly grown-up kids and a small, crazy dog.

Her first literary love was historical fiction, a genre which she relishes mixing up with romance and adventure in her own writing. Her most recent books are light, fun Regency romances written for Dragonblade Publishing: *The Imperial Season* series set at the Congress of Vienna; and the popular *Blackhaven Brides* series, which is set in a fashionable English spa town frequented by the great and the bad of Regency society.

Connect with Mary on-line – she loves to hear from readers:

Email Mary:
Mary@MaryLancaster.com

Website:
www.MaryLancaster.com

Newsletter sign-up:
http://eepurl.com/b4Xoif

Facebook:
facebook.com/mary.lancaster.1656

Facebook Author Page:
facebook.com/MaryLancasterNovelist

Twitter:
@MaryLancNovels

Amazon Author Page:
amazon.com/Mary-Lancaster/e/B00DJ5IACI

Bookbub:
bookbub.com/profile/mary-lancaster